ILLUSIONS OF LOVE

Jo Mattison is angry when her guardian decides to bequeath his property to whichever of her three cousins she chooses to marry — especially since Alec, whom she idolised throughout her childhood, makes a hasty exit with his girlfriend. Fleeing from the embarrassment of his defection, Jo goes to Borneo with her old friend Harry — but he has romantic illusions of his own . . . concerning Jo. When Alec follows them, Jo has a choice to make — but will it be the right one?

Books by Karen Abbott
in the Linford Romance Library:

KAREN ABBOTT

ILLUSIONS OF LOVE

Complete and Unabridged

LINFORD
Leicester

First published in Great Britain in 2007

First Linford Edition
published 2008

British Library CIP Data

Abbott, Karen
    Illusions of love.—Large print ed.—
    Linford romance library
    1. Love stories
    2. Large type books
    I. Title
    823.9′14 [F]

    ISBN 978–1–84782–146–1

Published by
F. A. Thorpe (Publishing)
Anstey, Leicestershire

Set by Words & Graphics Ltd.
Anstey, Leicestershire
Printed and bound in Great Britain by
T. J. International Ltd., Padstow, Cornwall

This book is printed on acid-free paper

1

'Well, Jo! Aren't you excited that your cousins are coming for the weekend, eh?' Willoughby Mattison challenged his adopted niece, the glimmer of fondness in this rheumy eyes belying the gruffness of his tone.

Jo Mattison instinctively glanced towards the window of her uncle's bedroom. It overlooked the front of Mattison Hall with its once-tailored gardens and the long sweeping drive that bisected them, though, from where she was seated at Willoughby's bedside, she couldn't see the shrub-lined drive, nor the lodge at its far end . . . but she knew that the imposing wrought iron gates would be standing wide open to welcome her three cousins as they arrived.

'I'm no longer a child, Uncle Willoughby,' she chided gently, turning to look at him. 'Nor are my cousins. We've all grown up and gone our different ways.'

'But you've still a fondness for them, haven't you?' Willoughby persisted. 'Inseparable, you were, you and the rest of *The Gang! The Famous Four* you called yourselves . . . and no-one would have known that one of you was a girl!'

He chuckled as his memory of those far-off days when Jo eagerly awaited the long holidays when Alec, Simon and Giles came to stay, filling the house with the noise of exuberant youth. There had been the inevitable squabbles, of course . . . many of them caused by Jo's insistence on being allowed to join in all the activities the boys planned.

'Aye, you and Alec were always at one another's throats, contending for leadership. But I think you would have been disappointed if you'd manage to displace him,' Willoughby added shrewdly. 'Simon and Giles had to be content with the lower ranks. Oh, and young Bretherton, too, once you had conceded to allow him into your gang . . . one of your victories over Alec and I think he thought you'd get too sweet on Harry and replace him as your idol!'

Jo was glad that the dimness of the room hid the blush that was rising up from her neck to her cheeks.

'I was sweet on neither of them,' she hastily denied, refusing to acknowledge the unrequited passion of her teenage years. 'Alec was far too bossy and Harry . . . '

'Not bossy enough, eh?'

Willoughby's eyes narrowed slightly as he reached out to touch her hand. 'And what about Simon and Giles? Did you have any special fondness for either of them?'

Jo tucked some strands of her rich chestnut hair behind her ear with her free hand. 'I was fond of them all,' she allowed lightly. 'We had some great times.'

Her expression softened as she, too, let her memory drift back to those childhood years. 'Magical, in fact. My life changed when you had adopted me and brought me here. I'll never forget it. I love it so much . . . the house, with all its nooks and crannies; the grounds . . . the orchard; the meadow and the woodland leading down to the river; and the back pastures going up into the moors. We had everything we needed for any adventure we dreamed up.' She sighed with contentment. 'I'll always love it . . . even when . . . '

Her voice faltered away and Willoughby took up her words.

'Even when I'm gone, you mean,' he said softly. He patted her hand. 'I know, my dear, I know. It's a pity the property is entailed and has to go to a male of my choice . . . and a pity, Joanna, you've no young man with serious intentions. How old are you? Twenty-two? And no-one in mind? You would be considered well and truly on the shelf in my young days!'

Jo forced a light-hearted laugh. 'We don't believe in rushing into marriage in the twenty-first century!' she declared.

'Besides, I like my job too much to want to settle down just yet. You know how thrilled I am with the British Wildlife Project I've just finished. There aren't many men who want to play second fiddle to a freelance wildlife photographer!'

'Maybe not . . . but I'd die a happier man if I knew you were settled down.'

Jo gathered his hand between both of hers and squeezed it. 'Don't talk about dying. You've got lots of years left. It's just this silly old dose of flu you've had that has left you a bit depressed. Why, you'll soon be gadding about in the garden again getting in Mr Thornton's way when he's brushing up the fallen leaves and driving Mrs Bretherton to despair when you're never in for your meals on time.'

'Maybe. Maybe. We'll see.' He patted her hand again, suddenly lighthearted and chuckling again. 'And don't you worry your pretty little head about me. You're right. I'm not dying yet . . . and I've thought of a way to die happy when

5

my time comes.'

Jo was glad that his gloomy mood had passed and exclaimed, 'Uncle Willoughby, you old rascal! Whatever do you mean? What are you up to?'

'Never you mind, Jo, my love! Now, go and tell Bretherton to come and see me. I'm tired and need to rest for an hour or so.'

His voice weakened and Jo was alarmed to see how pale his face had become. She stood up hastily. 'Shall I bring your lunch up later, Uncle Willoughby?'

He shook his head slightly, his eyes closing. 'No. You look after those nephews of mine when they deign to arrive . . . and remember to send them up to see me once lunch is over. I'll see them all together.'

On that enigmatic note, Willoughby sank deeper into his pillow and Jo could tell from his breathing that he had fallen asleep and so she tiptoed from the room.

Jo was glad to escape to the sanctity

of her own room in order to sort out her tumbling thoughts that Willoughby's comments had stirred into life. Like her uncle's room, it, too, overlooked the front of the house and she seated herself on the broad window seat and gazed out along the drive as she had done for as many years as she could remember when her cousins were due to arrive.

What were they making of their uncle's summons? She wasn't sure of his reason herself, apart from presuming it was a desire to see them all, brought on by his recent illness. Was he going to tell them which one he had chosen to inherit his home and the cluster of farms that made up his estate?

Which one would it be? Simon the son of the elder of his two sisters? Or Alec or Giles, who were the sons of his younger sister? Both of his sisters were many years younger than he, which was why he preferred to think of Jo as his niece, rather than an adopted daughter. It had put her on the same footing as his three nephews, apart from the fact that she lived at Mattison Hall whilst the boys only visited.

Alec was the eldest, five years her senior. He had always seemed grown-up to her, she mused. She must have been six or seven when she first singled him out from the others for her special notice. He could do no wrong in her eyes. He was tall and good-looking, even then, with dark brown hair that he liked to wear a bit longer than was fashionable. His total disregard of danger had made him a natural leader. It was Alec who had organised them into making a raft from felled branches in the wood . . . but it had fallen apart in the middle of the river and they had all got soaked . . . and grounded for two days!

Another time, they built a tree house in the wood, its only means of access up a precarious rope ladder, which Jo had mastered before Simon, who was three years older than her. As an only son, his mother doted on him and loud was her anguish whenever he returned to the house with his knees cut and bleeding or his clothes torn.

Giles was the youngest at twenty and had always been made aware of his lowly positions in the gang. His pride was salved when Harry Bretherton, the son of Willoughby's new housekeeping couple, and four years his senior, had joined the household. Harry had always been kept on the fringe of the gang, being allowed only a subsidiary membership, a position he had to earn by completing some daredevil tasks set by Alec.

Jo pursed her lips thoughtfully as she recalled how her friendship with Harry developed during her cousins' absence from the house in term times, but was always thrust aside when the gang was reunited, mainly, she ruefully admitted, due to her desire to become the 'apple of Alec's eye'!

It was Harry whom she had blatantly begged to teach her how to kiss after Alec's cool peck on her cheek at her sixteenth birthday party, when Alec

9

had admiringly whispered, 'You've started to grow up, little cousin,' before whisking away to dance with the long-legged blonde he had brought with him.

Her cheeks burned at the memory. The 'kissing lessons' had been rather enjoyable . . . but never put to their intended use as Alec had left university that summer and had started to work his way up through a firm of solicitors in Manchester. But she knew she still had hoped of becoming the special girl in his life . . . a position so far held temporarily by a non-ending succession of pretty blondes. Maybe the answer was to change the colour of her hair . . .

Simon and Giles then came less often and Harry had left as well. He had worked at Longleat for a number of years. Coincidentally, he too was due home this weekend, a farewell visit to his parents before going to Borneo to help set up a Rehabilitation Centre for orang-utans in the jungle. It would be good to have everyone under the same roof again, she reflected, even if only for a few hours.

She glanced through the window. No sign of anyone yet. Good. She had time to nip along to the kitchen to make sure Mrs Bretherton had everything in hand.

Simon and his mother were the first to arrive. Jo saw Simon's BMW coming sedately along the drive and was at the door to receive them by the time Simon had meticulously parked his car with all four wheels parallel to the edging that kept the chunky gravelled stones in place.

'Simon! Great to see you! Did you have a good journey!' She hugged him briefly, remembering to swiftly turn her cheek towards him to avoid his rather wet kiss being planted on her lips.

'Hi, Jo! You're looking lovely, as usual, isn't she, Mother?'

Jo looked past him into the interior of car and noticed for the first time that Simon's mother was seated within. She bobbed her head inside.

'And Auntie Iris! I didn't know you were coming too! How lovely to see you! Come on in. Mrs Bretherton will soon have a pot of tea ready!'

Iris returned her smile a little grimly. 'Well, let that dear boy of mine come round to help me get out and then I can go inside.'

Simon turned round the back of the car to open the front passenger door and held the crook of his right arm towards his mother to assist her as she struggled to get out of the passenger seat. Jo preceded them up the steps to hold open the door and then directed them into the living-room.

'Make yourselves comfortable. I'll let Mrs Bretherton know you are here.'

No sooner were they served with a tray of tea, coffee and biscuits than the sound of a high-powered motorbike made its presence felt outside the window and Jo rose to see a black-leather clad rider, oblivious to the trail of churned gravel that he had left in his wake, hauling his magnificent candy-red bike onto its stand. He was already bounding up the steps when Jo opened the door to welcome him. It was her younger cousin, Giles.

'Jo!' he exclaimed boisterously. 'Great to see you! What do you think of her, eh?'

He gesticulated to where his bike stood gleaming in the sunshine and Jo responded enthusiastically.

'Wicked!' she grinned. 'New, is it?'

'Only had it a week. Yamaha R1 1000cc! You should see it go. You'll have to have a ride on it. Care to come now?'

'Later,' Jo promised, noticing the spare helmet strapped to the pillion seat. 'Come inside first and have a cup of tea or coffee.'

'Right-ho!' He glanced at the parked BMW. 'That's Simon's is it? He's been splashing out! Spending his inheritance before he's got it, is he?'

'I wouldn't know about that,' Jo demurred, standing aside to let him into the hallway, thinking that Giles, too, had an extravagant mode of transport. 'He's a bit premature, if he is.'

'Oh-ho! You know something we don't, eh? Who's getting it, then?'

Jo felt irritated at his presumption. 'I've no idea,' she snapped. 'What I meant was Uncle Willoughby's not dead yet . . . and not likely to be so for years to come.'

'Now, now! Though I suppose it's understandable that you're a bit narked that you'll be excluded from inheriting because you're a girl. I expect whoever gets it will let you continue to live here if you want to. It's large enough.'

'I probably wouldn't want to . . . and, as I said, it won't be for years yet, so there's no point going on about it.'

Giles placed his crash helmet and leather gloves on the hall table and followed her into the living-room. 'Hi, Simon! How's things? Nice car you've got!' He dutifully leaned over to plant a brief kiss on Iris's cheek. 'Hi, Auntie Iris. You're looking great.'

Iris shuddered at his casual address

and regarded his leathers with some disdain. 'Good morning, Giles. Where's that brother of yours, Giles? Bothering to come, is he?'

'Oh, I should think so, Auntie Iris,' Giles grinned, unabashed by his aunt's obvious disapproval. 'You know what Alec is like. He'll be trying to decide which girl to bring.'

Jo felt a pang at Giles' suggestion, knowing that he was probably right. She was glad that her head was bowed over the coffee pot.

The merry tooting of a car horn outside the window diffused the uncomfortable atmosphere and Jo thankfully excused herself and hurried to the door.

Alec had swirled his bright red open-top sports car to a standstill amidst a flurry of gravel. He waved towards Jo.

'Hi, gorgeous!' he called as he athletically sprang over the top of his low-slung door. 'Hope I've not kept you waiting.'

He strode round the front of the car

to assist his passenger out of her seat. Jo's eyes narrowed slightly as the lithe blonde took hold of Alec's fingers and smoothly uncurled herself out of the passenger seat to stand beside Alec. Her tanned skin was barely covered by a skimpy pale blue dress. She looked stunning.

Jo waited on the top step as the handsome couple came forward, not trusting her legs to carry her down the short flight.

'Meet Marylea,' Alec said to her, grinning down at his companion. 'I thought she might brighten up Uncle Willoughby's day. Marylea, this is my little cousin, Joanna, known to one and all as Jo.'

'Not so little!' Jo protested as Alec eyed her up and down. She dragged her eyes away from Alec's scrutiny and smiled at Marylea. 'Hello, Marylea. Welcome to Mattison Hall.'

'Not so little, indeed,' Alec agreed softly as he and Marylea arrived beside her. 'You've done some growing up since I last saw you, Jo.'

He lifted her chin and kissed her unprepared lips, sending a frisson of surprised delight coursing through her body . . . It was all she had ever dreamed it would be.

2

Jo had to summon all her willpower to resist the overwhelming urge to lean towards Alec and let the strength of his body support her trembling limbs. Instead, she pulled away with a nervous laugh, taking a step backwards as they broke contact.

'C . . . Come and meet the others, Marylea,' she stammered, agitatedly tucking a strand of hair behind her ear. 'Giles is here. You'll have seen his motorbike,' she rushed on. 'And Simon has brought Auntie Iris.'

'Still the same 'mummy's boy'?' Alec commented, unashamedly grinning at her discomposure. He winked as he passed her, but Jo turned away sharply and led the way along the hall to the living-room door, stepping aside to allow Alec and Marylea to pass in front of her. She was very conscious of the closeness of Alec's body as he passed by but she stood resolutely still when he gently flicked his finger against her hot cheek.

'Keep growing up,' he whispered teasingly, 'and who knows what might happen.'

Jo felt her heart leap at the thought of the promise of her long-held hopes coming to fruition . . . but she didn't like the fact that he would flirt with her whilst being with another girl.

An undercurrent of tension hovered over the luncheon table, coming mainly from Auntie Iris and Alec, Jo realised. It made her feel edgy.

'All we need is Harry to complete the gang!' she said in a misguided attempt to fill an uncomfortable void.

'Harry?' Auntie Iris queried, as if she had never heard of him.

'The Bretherton's boy who became our lowly subaltern,' Alec drawled laconically towards her, before directing his gaze at Jo. 'Now, what need do we have of him, Jo? Aren't we Mattisons sufficient for you?' He grinned sideways at Simon and Giles. '*The Mattison Might!*' he declared powerfully, raising his hand towards the others.

Giles, Simon and even Jo stretched out their right arms across the table and clasped their hands over Alec's.

'*The Mattison Might!*' they echoed in unison, exchanging triumphant grins.

'Oh, you and your gang!' Marylea complained. 'Honestly, Alec went on and on about it on the journey here. And his name isn't even Mattison. None of you have the name.'

'I have!' Jo declared.

'But only by adoption, dear,' Auntie Iris said pointedly. 'I'm the only true Mattison here . . . '

'Ah, but the Mattison blood is in our veins, Auntie Iris!' Alec declared with some satisfaction. 'And one of us, no doubt, will be willing to change his name back to Mattison, eh, lads, should the need arise!'

'Speaking of which, isn't it time we went to see Uncle Willoughby?' Simon suggested, looking at his mother for approval.

Iris deposited her napkin on the table and pushed back her chair. 'Yes, dear, you're right. I do hope Willoughby hasn't got anything infectious, Joanna. Has his room been well-sprayed with disinfectant? I don't want to catch any of his germs.'

No, all you want to catch is his money, Jo thought angrily as she too rose to her feet. 'Uncle Willoughby only wants to see his nephews,' she reminded her aunt. To her cousins, she added, 'Ask Mrs Bretherton to see if he's awake and ready to see you.'

'But I want to see him myself,' Iris protested, as the three young men left the room. 'After all, I am his sister. He should have asked to see me first. I could advise him on whom to choose.'

Any reply Jo might have made was interrupted by a quiet knock at the door and when it opened, Jo beamed with delight.

'Harry!' she exclaimed, leaping up

from her seat and crossing the room to greet the tall fair-haired man hesitating in the doorway with a friendly hug. 'It's great to see you. Come on in. You remember Simon's mother, Auntie Iris, don't you? And this is Marylea, a . . . er . . . friend of Alec's,' she ended lamely, knowing Harry's opinion of Alec's quick changeover of girlfriends.

Harry stepped further into the room and politely acknowledged both ladies, but swiftly returned his attention to Jo.

'I'm sorry to interrupt,' he apologised, 'but I didn't want to leave without seeing you.'

'Oh! I thought you were here overnight,' Jo exclaimed with disappointment. 'I hoped we might see each other later.'

'So did I,' Harry rejoined, 'but there's been a last-minute change of plan. My photographer has taken ill and can't come with me. I've got to get a replacement immediately if I'm not to waste the tickets on tomorrow morning's flight. I've just been chatting to

Mum and Dad and now I'm going to the lodge to pack my things and make a few phone calls. Then as soon as we've had dinner, I'll have to be off, I'm afraid.'

Jo realised that she was going to miss him more than she had thought she would. He would be the other side of the world instead of the other end of the country. There were lots of things she wanted to ask him about his new job and whether or not he thought a project in Longleat might be a feasible opportunity for her to attempt.

She made a snap decision. 'Auntie Iris? Marylea? Would you mind if I slip away for quarter-of-an-hour or so? I feel bad about deserting you, but I would like to talk to Harry about something before he goes.'

When Iris imperiously waved her hand indicating that she went, and Marylea casually shrugged her consent, Jo grabbed Harry's arm and pulled him out of the room.

'I'll walk back to the lodge with you,'

she suggested, grabbing hold of her jacket as she passed by the hall-stand and slipping it on. 'I want to hear all about your job in Borneo. What will you be doing?'

'I'll be helping to build up a rehabilitation centre where they care for orphaned orang-utans and train them how to fend for themselves when they are released back into the jungle,' Harry explained as they left the house and began to saunter across the grass towards the lodge.

'Mike Rowlinson, the manager has had an accident and is in hospital and they need a zoologist to help with the programme. I've been out there before and know the area . . . and I have a special interest in orang-utans. So, I volunteered and, fortunately for me, my boss at Longleat was willing to sponsor me for six months, so, although I'll be working for a pittance, I'll have enough to live on.'

'It sounds exciting. But, why do you need a photographer?'

'They want to record what they are doing to help to advertise the centre and, hopefully, get more people to sponsor the work, like they do at Sepilok, a well-established rehabilitation centre about forty or fifty miles away, nearer the east coast. I worked there for a while when I was out there before, so I have some ideas about what is needed and what will appeal to new sponsors.'

He stopped and took hold of both her arms above the elbows. 'But, what about you, Jo? You look a bit run-down after your spell of looking after your uncle. Are you sure you haven't been overdoing it? Mum said you took turns with Dad day and night whilst Willoughby was at his worst. You ought to be thinking of taking a few weeks off now that your Wild-Life project is finished.'

Jo could see his concern for her in his eyes and she nodded in agreement.

'I will . . . but I need to be setting up what I'm going to do next. I wondered about doing something at Longleat. Can you use your influence and make enquiries for me? I know you're going away, but a quick phone call might be all that's needed. I'll be willing to show them my portfolio and the project I've just finished.' She smiled beguilingly. 'I'll be your best friend and invite you to my next party.'

Harry grinned as she chanted the familiar childhood phrase. 'Liar! I know who you'd like for your 'best friend'. I saw him on his way upstairs with Simon and Giles.'

His grin faded and he took hold of her shoulders, looking seriously into her eyes. 'Give up on him, Jo. He isn't worthy of you.'

Seeing the hurt in her eyes, he lightened his tone. 'I bet he hasn't even kissed you yet . . . in spite of the practice you inveigled me into giving you.'

Embarrassed by his reminder and the near truth of what he was saying, Jo was stung into retorting, 'Yes, he has. And he said he'll be asking me out soon

. . . as soon as he's finished with Marylea.'

As soon as she had said those words Jo wished she hadn't. It wasn't true. She had twisted and exaggerated what Alec had actually said.

Harry's hand fell from her shoulders and his face looked sorrowful. 'You're a fool, Jo . . . and you know it. He'll play with you for a while and then drop you, like he's dropped all the others. And I don't know what you'll do if he inherits this place.'

He looked at her thoughtfully. 'Is that why you want him so badly? Because you think Mattison Hall will be his?' He shook his head. 'It won't be enough, Jo. A house can't bind you together. You need love for that.'

'And you'd know all about that, would you?' Jo retorted. 'How many girlfriends have you had? None that I know of.'

'No serious ones — and you know the reason why. But I think I've just woken up to the reality of the situation.

You're in love with a house, not a person. Well, I haven't got a house, Jo, except for a rented one. And, for the next six months, I won't even have that. But you can keep your house and your one-sided love affair with Alec. I'm through waiting for you to grow up and come to your senses.'

Jo shivered at the raw anger in his face. She shouldn't have taunted him. She knew he thought himself in love with her . . . a love she was unable to return because she was besotted with Alec.

'I'm sorry, Harry,' she whispered, reaching her hand out towards him.

Harry flinched away, his face looking grim. 'I'm sorry we have to part like this, Jo . . . but I don't see any point in you coming any further.'

'Harry . . . ?'

He held up his hand to stop her protest. 'I'll get you an interview at Longleat . . . and I wish you all the best at it . . . but I think for now, we'd better say good-bye.'

Jo's throat felt too tight to speak. She knew that if she managed to speak she would also cry and her pride forbade that. And so, holding back the sob that threatened to erupt, she turned on her heels and ran back to the house.

Harry watched until she was out of sight. He closed his eyes to shut out the memory of her anguished expression, slamming his right fist into his left palm.

Jo was halfway up the front steps when the door opened. Not wanting to face anyone until she had rinsed her face, she abruptly halted and turned to dart away, but Giles's voice called out to her.

'There you are, Jo! We wondered when you'd be back!'

He glanced a bit warily over his shoulder and pulled the door closed behind him. 'How about coming for that ride on my bike?' he asked, as he drew on his leather gloves.

He took hold of her elbow and drew her down the steps with him, seemingly unaware that her eyes were wet with unshed tears. He unstrapped the spare helmet and held it out to her.

'You'll be quite safe. Auntie Iris might not think much of me, but I don't take risks with this beauty!' he said, possessively stroking his hand along the bike.

Giles turned to unlock the safety chain and haul the huge machine off its stand. He sat astride it and started the engine while Jo put the helmet on and fastened the strap under her chin.

'On you get,' he commanded over the engine's roar.

With a surge that almost tipped her backwards, the motorbike leapt forward, scattering gravel in all directions. Jo hung on tightly, leaning against Giles's back, tucking her head sideways against his shoulders as they sped around the curve of the drive and into the straight length leading to the gates. With the man of her dreams it would have been a curiously intimate posture . . . but as it was . . .

It was a thrilling ride. The steady throb of power excited her senses and she forgot everything except the need to remain balanced as they swooped around the bends in the road. Giles was an accomplished biker and, although they were travelling fast, Jo felt perfectly safe. It was just what she needed to banish the distress caused by her quarrel with Harry.

By the time Giles was once more pulling up just short of the front steps of Mattison Hall, Jo was feeling reasonably composed. She carefully dismounted, her legs trembling a little from the thrill of the ride.

'That was great!' she exclaimed, as she unbuckled her helmet, glad to have had a respite before facing everybody. 'Thanks, Giles. We must do it again sometime.'

She held out the helmet to him but, instead of taking it, Giles took hold of her wrist. 'I'm thinking of touring abroad on my bike this summer. How about you coming along? You'd enjoy it?' After a slight hesitation, he rushed on, 'We always got on well together, Jo, didn't we? Especially with us being the youngest two of the gang. Why don't we surprise everyone and get hitched? We'd make a good team. How about it, eh?'

Jo stared at him, stunned into silence. She shook her head in bewilderment. 'Giles . . . ?'

'We could go right now and get married abroad somewhere,' Giles continued, oblivious to the shock his words were causing. 'What d'you say?'

Convinced he was joking, Jo laughed. 'I say, 'On your bike, lad!' I've no intentions of getting married . . . not yet. Not for a long time. And certainly not to . . . '

'A fool like me?' Giles anticipated with a wry twist of his mouth.

Jo laid her hand on his arm. 'No . . . you're not a fool, Giles . . . but it would be foolish to rush into marriage like that. We had good times together when we were kids, but that was years ago. We hardly know each other now.

Go on your tour . . . and enjoy it.'

Giles looked slightly abashed . . . but not too upset by her words, 'Ah, well! It was worth a try! Sorry, Jo. No hard feelings, eh?'

Still puzzled by his out-of-character proposal, Jo shook her head. 'Of course not. Are you coming back inside before you go?'

'No, I may as well be off. I've said goodbye to the others.' He took the helmet out of her hand and twisted round to fasten it to the seat behind him. Then, after a wry salute with his gloved hand, he slipped into gear, turned in a wide circle and roared off along the drive.

Shaking her head in bemused wonder, Jo watched until he was out of sight, wondering whatever had brought on a proposal of marriage. Giles and her? What a mis-matched couple they would have made.

She was still smiling in a bemused fashion when she walked into the living-room. She was surprised to see only

Auntie Iris and Simon seated there and detected an unmistakeable air of tension. Simon leaped to his feet as if from a spring . . . but then stood uncertainly.

'Jo, you're back. Did Giles . . .'

'Did Giles give you a safe ride on that monstrous machine?' Auntie Iris demanded, quelling Simon's words with her imperious tones.

'Why, y . . . yes. It was . . . good. Er . . . Is Alec still with Uncle Willoughby? Where's Marylea? What did . . . ?'

'Alec and Marylea have gone,' Iris replied before Jo had completed her question. 'He seemed anxious to get away, though I told him he ought to wait to say goodbye to you. However, he never did put much store on good manners . . . unlike Simon here.' She bestowed a motherly smile of pride on her son. 'Such a considerate boy. He thinks very highly of you, Jo. He always has.'

Iris rose to her feet and patted Jo's hand. 'I'll just leave the two of you alone for a few minutes while I go to see dear Willoughby . . . and, then we, too, must be on our way. Unless of course . . . No, I'll say no more of that.' And, with what seemed to be a 'knowing look' at Simon, she left the room.

Jo stared at the closed door and then back to Simon. 'What's going on, Simon? What did Uncle Willoughby say to you boys? Has he chosen his heir?'

Simon shook his head. 'No, he said . . . '

He stopped abruptly and seemed to galvanise himself into action. Taking Jo by surprise, he swiftly closed the distance between them and took hold of both her hands.

'Jo, I didn't realise how much you mean to me . . . but seeing you again today after a couple of years apart, has made me realise what a fine girl you are and how much I feel about you.'

'Simon!' Jo warned with a bemused laugh, trying to pull her hands free, somehow sensing what was coming . . . but Simon held on to her and hurriedly

continued, 'What I mean to say is . . . I
. . . er . . . think you are a wonderful girl
and I hope very much you will make
me the . . . er . . . happiest of men and
. . . er . . . agree to become my wife!
There!'

He almost sighed with relief, now
that his hurried speech was over and
looked totally woebegone when Jo
finally dragged her hands out of his
grip, her laughter now banished and her
expression furious.

'Do you think I'm stupid, or
something?' she demanded angrily,
advancing upon him with the first
finger of her right hand jabbing at his
chest. 'You've no wish to marry me. We
would drive each other crazy within the
first week. So, what's this all about, eh?'
jabbing him again.

Simon backed away from her, stum-
bling against a chair and skirting
narrowly past it. He managed to get
hold of the chair back and swiftly pulled
the chair between them, still backing
away, pulling the chair with him.

'You had no thoughts of wanting to marry me when you arrived here today. And you never have had,' Jo continued, reaching across the chair but no longer able to reach him. 'So, what's changed, eh?'

Simon looked like a hunted animal held at bay, his eyes darting from side to side looking for a way to escape. Jo took pity on him. She dropped her arm and faced him with the back of her hands resting on her hips.

'OK, Simon. Come clean. Auntie Iris put you up to that, didn't she? 'Simon thinks very highly of you'' she mimicked Iris's words. 'So, you've made your proposal and I've turned you down. Now, shall we start again.'

3

Simon had the grace to look ashamed. 'You're right. Mother said I'd to ask you to marry me . . . before one of the others got in first. She was fuming when Giles whisked you off on his bike like that. She said he was sure to get in first. He didn't did he?'

Jo laughed dryly. 'He did! But with no more success that you. Honestly, Simon. What's got into you both? There's never been a romantic moment between us. Believe me, by the time you and Giles arrive home you'll both be relieved that I've turned you down.'

'I'm relieved already,' he said with a weak grin. 'I told mother it was a stupid idea, but she wouldn't give up on it. Er . . . Will you tell her I did it and that you were . . . er . . . impressed a little? She might believe you,' he added lamely.

Jo snorted her disgust as his weakness of character. 'Simon! You are the limit. You let Auntie Iris rule your life. It's time you broke loose and lived a little. But, why on earth did you both propose to me today?'

As Simon hesitated to reply, Jo's eyes narrowed slightly as a thought occurred to her. 'Just what did Uncle Willoughby say to you guys? He's behind this, isn't he? Come on, out with it.'

Simon looked as if he were caught between the devil and the deep blue sea, wondering which adversary he could afford to offend — the one present or the one upstairs in his sickbed. With Jo advancing towards him once more, her eyes glinting with hardly suppressed fury, he took the option of appeasing the one who was present. He tried to shrug carelessly as he said uneasily, 'Er . . . Uncle Willoughby said he would leave his property to whoever . . . er, one of us . . . you agreed to marry.'

'And you agreed to that, you

low-lives?' Jo said incredulously, halting in her tracks. 'Wasn't there one of the three of you who would stand up to him and tell him what you thought of this humiliating idea?'

Simon held out his hands, palms outwards as if fending off a blow. 'Alec laughed. He thought it was a hoot. We, er, didn't know what to say.'

Jo curtailed her threatening attitude and put the backs of her hands onto her hips. 'Well, I know what to say to him. Just watch me.'

With no more ado, she leaped up the wide staircase and thundered along the landing to her uncle's bedroom. Auntie Iris was just coming out of it and she hastily stepped aside as Jo whirled past her into the room and marched over towards the bed, where she stood with her hands on her hips looking angrily at her uncle.

'Well, you've done it, this time, Uncle Willoughby! How dare you offer me as a 'lure' . . . a bribe almost! You might as well have put me up for auction to the highest bidder! Well, I've turned down the two who offered! Alec . . . ' Her voice almost broke at the thought of the humiliation, ' . . . didn't even wait to take his chance. He's high-tailing it home as fast as he can. You've made it impossible . . . '

Her anger drained away and silent tears ran down her cheeks as she turned her head away.

Willoughby lifted his hand towards her, but when she ignored it, he let it fall down again into the counterpane. 'I told them not to tell you. You weren't supposed to know.'

Jo's head jerked to face him again. 'And that's supposed to make me feel better, is it? What I didn't know wouldn't hurt me.' She fought back a lump in her throat and added, 'Well, your three nephews have failed your task, so what are you going to do now?'

'Look, I didn't . . . '

Jo pressed her lips together. 'Don't try and wriggle out of it. It's too late for that.' She whirled round to face Iris, remembering Iris's willingness to play along with the scheme . . . as long as her son was the winner. 'You'd better make arrangements to stay and look after Uncle Willoughby, Auntie Iris, because I'm off!'

She stalked towards the door but was halted by Willoughby's feeble voice. 'Don't go, Jo! Not like this. What if Alec comes back? What shall I tell him?'

'Tell him whatever you like, Uncle Willoughby!' she said over her shoulder. 'I don't see why you should suddenly need me to tell you what to say. You seem to have had enough ideas of your own until now.'

Iris put out a hand to restrain Jo as she stalked past her. 'You can't leave, Joanna! Think of your uncle!' she wailed. 'Think of Simon! Have you really given thought to what you are doing? Ask her again, Simon! Tell her you love her!'

Jo laughed. She flung a mocking glance at Simon, who was still hovering outside the room. 'He did, Auntie Iris! I seem to remember that he did! But I don't love him! At least, not like that!'

'You're an ungrateful hussy, that's what you are!' Iris snapped. 'After all my brother has done for you, you're abandoning him in his hour of need! Simon, you're well out of it. She would have led you a merry dance, I can see!'

Jo raised an eyebrow and grinned at Simon. ''Hussy', eh? I'm not entirely sure what that means . . . but I take it that it isn't a compliment. And I already told him that he's better off without me. We're in agreement at last, Auntie Iris.'

She paused in the doorway and looked back at her uncle's form in the huge bed. Her temper had drained away now and she merely felt saddened by the whole incident. 'Goodbye, Uncle Willoughby. I *will* come back . . . eventually. But you'll have to make your choice without me in the equation.'

She hesitated, taking pity on her uncle's desolate expression. Suddenly overcome by the way things had turned, she rushed back to the bed and clasped Willoughby's hand.

'I still love you, but I couldn't bear to hang around . . . waiting. You *must* understand that. Nor to keep fending off proposals from my other two cousins. I'll write and let you know where I am, I promise.'

She rushed to her room and hauled a suitcase from the top of her wardrobe, hastily cramming as many clothes into it as she could, regardless of whether or not they were suitable. What else?

Her laptop was in its case and her photographic equipment in another. She opened a locked drawer and grabbed a handful of personal papers and stuffed them into a small backpack that she frequently used when casually dressed, and then took a lingering look around her room.

An overwhelming sense of humiliation swept over her again and, choking back a sob, she snatched up her belongings and hurried downstairs. She hoped that Simon or Iris wouldn't try to stop her . . . and they didn't.

Not wanting to face Mrs Bretherton or her husband in the kitchen, Jo left by the front door and then slipped around to the back to where her white Renault Clio was parked. She'd need to get petrol somewhere and decide where to stop overnight. Tears were running freely down her cheeks and she frequently wiped the back of her hand across them, brushing them away, angry with herself for caring so much. She was glad to be going! She was!

But not like this, she inwardly whispered.

She was coming out of the last bend in the drive, driving much faster than was wise at this point, when a car . . . Harry's car, she realised without making a conscious identification . . . emerged from the side of the lodge and headed towards her. He should have been going the other way, towards the road! Why was he heading up the drive? Had someone phoned to the lodge and asked him to stop her?

Her erratic driving had taken her too far over the middle of the drive. Two cars *could* pass in safety, but generally at a slower speed. With a stab of panic, she wrenched at the steering wheel trying to pull over to her left, but she wrenched too hard and her car spun off the road onto the grass verge.

She stamped on the brakes . . . and although she wrenched the wheel back to her right, it was too late. In a sequence of slow-motion film-frames, she saw the ranch-style fencing that bordered the drive lurch towards her but, before she crashed into it, her car dropped nose-down into the wide grass ditch that ran alongside it.

Her seatbelt jerked and her body rocked forward and back again, the back of her head being thrown against her headrest. Steam was arising from the crumpled bonnet of her car, but she was too stunned to take it in. The door at the side of her was wrenched open.

'Are you all right, Jo? Come on, let's

get you out of there! Can you unfasten your seatbelt?'

It was Harry.

She moved her legs and wriggled her feet. 'Y . . . yes, I think so.'

'Good! Then, come on. I'll help you out.'

It was a bit of a struggle, with the car being at a crazy angle, but Harry managed to help her onto the grass verge. Her legs wouldn't hold her up and she sank down onto the grass at Harry's feet. Immediately, he crouched down beside her.

'Where were you going? There's nothing gone wrong up at the house, has it? Is your uncle OK?'

'Huh! He's in fine form! No, I just . . . '

What could she say? She didn't want to further humiliate herself, though, no doubt, he would get to know from someone.

'I just decided to go away. Auntie Iris will look after Uncle Willoughby for a while.'

'Well, you'll not be going far in your car for a while,' Harry pointed out. 'As well as needing to be pulled out of the ditch, I wouldn't be surprised if you've busted the radiator. And maybe damaged the exhaust system.'

'Oh, no!' Jo bit her lower lip. 'I really do want to get away tonight.' She looked up at Harry hopefully. 'I don't suppose . . . Would you give me a lift somewhere? Manchester would do.'

'Sure. What about your car, though? You just can't leave it like that.'

'Will you ask your dad to see to it for me. I'm sure Uncle Willoughby will reimburse him.'

'No problem.' He stood to his feet. 'Your luggage is in the back, is it?'

'Yes.'

Harry easily swung the luggage into the back of his own car and Jo got into the passenger seat.

'I've left your keys in the car,' Harry said as he seated himself beside her a few minutes later, 'and I've phoned Dad and asked him to get Bert from

Black's Garage to come out and take your car away. Now, let's get this car heading in the right direction and we'll be on our way.'

As he reversed back as far as the lodge and swung round into the parking space beside it, Jo said hesitantly. 'Why were you heading towards the house?'

Harry glanced sideways at her. 'To come and make up with you, of course. I couldn't go away and leave things as they were. Friends again, are we?'

'Of course. I'm sorry for the way I spoke to you. I was out of order.'

'We both were. I'm sorry, too. I value your friendship, Jo, whatever happens.'

They were speeding along the road now, but Harry took his eyes off the road long enough to exchange grins with Jo. Satisfied that all was well between them now, she settled back against her seat.

'Did you get hold of a photographer?' she asked after a short silence.

'Not yet. I've got someone else in mind to contact when I get to

Manchester, but I'm pushing my luck a bit, now. He'll just have to come out later, as soon as he can arrange it. Where are you heading for? I don't think you said.'

'I didn't. I'm not sure yet. I did wonder about following up my idea of doing a project at Longleat. Did you have time to put in a phone call for me?'

'Not yet . . . sorry. Remind me again before I drop you off at Manchester. Are you going to put up overnight somewhere? You could have the sofa in my flat, if you wish.'

'Great! Thanks, Harry! I'll take you up on that. Unless . . . '

She drew her breath in sharply as an idea popped into her mind — but would Harry agree? Her heart seemed to leap up within her as she put her startling idea into words.

'Harry? I could be your photographer. What do you say?'

4

Jo held her breath as the powerful thrust of the engines of the Boeing 747 pressed her back against her seat as the huge aircraft thundered along the runway — and then they were swiftly soaring into the morning sky. Jo was in the window seat and she gazed down at the rapidly shrinking landscape below them.

'Fantastic!' she breathed, clicking away with her camera. Thank goodness she had scooped up her passport from her wardrobe when she was hastily packing her suitcase.

Not that it had been easy to persuade Harry to agree to take her with him as his photographer. For a while, she was certain he was going to refuse — and could she blame him after the way she had spoken to him earlier? But he did agree — finally . . . because his other contact was already busy on an assignment somewhere else.

With a contented sigh, Jo leaned back against her seat again to settle down to a twelve-hour flight to Kuala Lumpur and the connection to Kota Kinabalu in Sabah, Malaysian Borneo, a few hours later.

Harry reclined his seat and closed his eyes, but Jo was too fraught to do likewise. She couldn't help wondering what Uncle Willoughby was thinking. She hoped the shock of her departure wouldn't damage his recovery progress, but he had brought it on himself, she reasoned.

At the International airport at Kuala Lumpur, they had a light meal as they waited for their flight to Kota Kinabalu to be called. By this time, Jo's mind and body knew that she had missed most of a complete night's sleep . . . and in spite of the fact her eyes and other senses told her it was mid-morning, she fell asleep leaning against Harry's shoulder, unaware that she snuggled cosily into the familiar contours of his body.

She dreamed that Alec was looking for her, but couldn't find her and, when the sound of someone's voice saying her name penetrated into her dream, she murmured, 'I'm here, Alec.'

'Wake up, Jo! It's Harry . . . and it's time to go.' Harry's voice spoke lightly above her head. 'Our flight to Sabah has been called.'

She was aware of a sense of disappointment as she pushed herself into a sitting position. Alec had seemed so real.

Harry stood up and was busily picking up their flight bags as Jo scrambled to her feet and sleepily took her bag from him. The sense of Alec's nearness was fading fast and she wanted to retreat into her dream to hold on to him, but she knew it was impossible.

Two-and-a-half hours later her eyes were burning through lack of sleep and her head felt muzzy, but excitement at their imminent landing was kicking in and Jo felt euphoric. She gazed through the window in rapt delight as the plane descended out of the clouds over the rainforest of Sabah.

Harry hauled their flight bags out of the overhead compartments and handed Jo hers.

'It's raining,' he warned, as he peered through the window.

'It'll be warm rain!' Jo quipped, refusing to be daunted by something so trivial. She accepted the brightly coloured umbrella as she stepped onto the tarmac and held it over her head as she quickened her pace towards the shelter of the building.

Half-an-hour later they were through the security checks, had collected their luggage from the carousel and taken possession of the four-wheel-drive truck that Harry had arranged to collect at the airport.

'We're on our way,' he grinned at Jo. 'Take a good look at that map the guy gave us and give me directions as we go.

We're heading for . . . there!' pointing at a red asterisk sited in what seemed to be the centre of the rainforest.

They soon left the comforting signs of modern town-life behind them and were driving along roads that were lined with an ever-increasing abundance of greenery. Giant twisted trees with hanging lianas twining among them crowded around them, barely visible through the spray and mist.

The stream of rain that still lashed against the windscreen and the regular motion of the wipers had a hypnotic effect. Jo was finding it difficult to keep her attention on the map and the road and her eyelids grew heavy.

The jolting of the truck jerked her awake. Her head felt as though it belonged to someone else. 'Where are we?'

She peered through the windscreen. The metalled surface had been left behind and they were now driving up a steep earthen, rocky track. In better weather, it would be hard-packed but today it was like a shallow, muddy river bubbling over an indeterminate surface.

'We're nearly there,' Harry murmured, leaning forward, intent on keeping the vehicle upright. 'Only another two or three miles, I think.'

It felt as though they were driving through a dark green tunnel as the jungle trees and creepers strove to reclaim the ground that had been taken from them. Jo twisted her head to try to see if she could see any sky above the canopy.

What she did see was a huge tree just ahead to the left, slowly tilting towards the track, snapping off branches of smaller trees that were in its path as it crashed downwards with accelerating speed.

'Brake!' she yelled, slapping the map in her hand down on the dashboard in unconscious memory of Harry's method of teaching her how to do emergency stops on her uncle's estate.

Harry instinctively did as she had commanded and they both lurched forward in their seats until restrained by their seatbelts. Their heads rocked back against their headrests and they stared aghast through the windscreen as the massive tree crashed almost on top of them, its branches buckling the radiator and metal bonnet of their vehicle and some scraping against the windshield.

Harry swallowed hard. 'I owe you one, Jo!' he said, still stunned. 'I didn't see it. We could have been killed.'

'Nothing wrong with your reactions, anyway!' Jo laughed tremulously. 'At least we're not completely underneath it. What shall we do now?'

'Let's get out and see what the damage is. It might still be drivable.'

He switched off the engine and they both jumped down into the ankle deep water, unmindful of the still-falling rain and silently surveyed the damage to the front of the truck.

The creatures of the rainforest seemed to have been startled into silence by the sudden event and as Jo stared around at the dripping greenery, she could imagine a hundred unseen eyes watching. Even as the thought occurred to her, the shrieks, calls and hums began to arise around them, bringing the jungle to life again.

'I wonder what made it fall just then?' Jo mused, staring at where it had come from, its path evident by the broken branches it had taken with it in its fall.

'It must have been weakened in last night's storm that the guy at the airport mentioned,' Harry supposed, his attention focused on the truck. 'Maybe the vibrations from our approach set it off on its final descent?'

He straightened up. 'The wipers are gone . . . wrenched out of their sockets. I can't see much else. I'll see if I can back the truck off the tree. Get ready to spot if any branches are caught up anywhere underneath and raise your hand if you want me to stop.'

'Hang on! I'll take a few photographs,' Jo decided. 'You never know. We may need them for insurance purposes. I suppose we are covered by insurance, are we?'

'I reckon so. It'll be in the paper work that guy gave us.'

Harry stood back whilst Jo took a few photographs of the scene from various angles. They wouldn't be the best of photographs, but they would give an accurate picture of the occurrence. When Jo was satisfied she had the best possible shots of the situation, Harry climbed back into the truck and started the engine again. Cautiously slipping the gear into reverse, he put pressure on the accelerator and slowly dragged the vehicle out of the clutches of the many branches that held it. The bent and buckled bonnet came into view and then the front of the radiator. Jo could see the front bumper about to be pulled of its brackets.

'Easy!' she called, raising her hand. She bent down to look underneath and eased out some small branches. 'OK! Back off again!'

Once clear of the tree, Harry switched

off the engine and joined Jo, who was busily photographing the buckled radiator and bonnet. He put his hand underneath feeling for the damage.

'There's hot water dripping down. I think the radiator's had it. It's been punctured somewhere,' he said as he straightened up. 'I'd better telephone the hire firm for advice.'

He found the relevant number but, when he tried to ring, there was no response. He frowned at his phone.

'There's no signal,' he said, glancing around at the impenetrable forest. 'We must be in a ravine.' He glanced again at the ordnance map. 'Yes, we are.' He twisted his mouth ruefully. 'It looks like we've got a walk ahead of us. It won't be too hard a trek . . . and it's certainly nearer than going back.'

He looked down at Jo's feet. 'Those sandals are worse than useless! Did you bring hiking boots?'

'No. I didn't know I would need them,' Jo said defensively, adding. 'I've got trainers.'

'Then you had better put them on, they'll be better than those.'

Harry went to the rear of the truck and let down the tailgate. He hauled out his large backpack and rummaged inside for his heavy hiking boots.

'First chance you get of going back to town, you'd better see if you can get some boots . . . and some rainwear,' he added as he perched on the tailgate and changed into his boots.

'Yes, Boss!' Jo quipped, perching beside him, glancing at him with mild irritation. 'You didn't used to be this bossy!' she complained, pushing her foot into a trainer and tying the lace. 'I hope you don't think I'm going to jump at every command!'

Harry laughed dryly. 'I wouldn't dare to be so optimistic! You were never very good at obeying orders . . . not even Alec's!'

'No,' she agreed with a sidelong grin. 'Well, as the only girl, I had to look out for myself, didn't I? I had to prove I was as good as you lads.'

Jo hastily transferred some jeans, shorts, tops and underwear from her suitcase to her flight bag and slung it over her back, adding the bag that contained the rest of her photographic equipment as well.

'And these bottles of water!' Harry said, forcing them into her side pockets. 'Let's finish this two-litre bottle before we set off.

'At least it's stopped raining,' she commented, as she wiped her lips on the back of her hand before handing the bottle back again. 'But the mozzies are out in force!'

Harry pulled a roll-on mosquito repellent out of a side pocket of his backpack. 'You're right! We need this!'

He took the top off and began to roll the liquid over Jo's arms and then went around her neck.

Jo was unaccountably aware of his closeness. He had changed in the years that they hadn't seen much of each other. He was more assertive and more . . . Jo searched her mind for the right word. More . . . masculine? Was that it? Not that he had ever been less than a rough and tumble lad . . . but, in his maturity, there was a sensuality about him that she had never been aware of before.

Jo felt confused. She didn't want him to attract her sensuously. He was her pal. Alec was the one who set her senses racing, not Harry! Aware that he was about to drop down and apply the roller to her legs, she hastily stepped back,

'I'll do that!' She took the roller out of his hand and quickly ran it over the exposed parts of her legs, happy to put some distance between them. Her heart was racing and her hands shaking. It must be the lack of sleep that was making her suddenly super-sensitive towards him, she reasoned.

When her legs were suitably pro-tected, she handed the roller back to him, making no offer to apply it for him and watched as he ran the roller over the exposed skin of his arms, his legs and lastly, his face and neck, still uncomfortably aware of his sensuality.

'You forgot your face,' Harry said, as he completed his own protection.

He stepped forward and, before Jo could take the roller from him, he took hold of her chin and turned her face away from him and lightly ran the roller down the side of her face near her hairline, gently lifting her hair out of the way.

'Now, the other side,' he said briskly.

Jo turned her face the other way, holding her breath now that they were so close again. She, aware that her heart had resumed its former thudding and, when Harry released his light hold of her, she hardly dared turn to face him, wondering if the panic she was feeling was evident to him.

For a moment, their eyes met and held and Jo was sure that he was going to kiss her. She remembered his kisses . . . surrogate kisses for Alec she had regarded them at the time, but her lips parted as they forgot the surrogacy and began to tingle with expectation.

Harry laughed as he dabbed the roller on the tip of her nose. 'All done!' he grinned. 'Time to go! And add 'jungle juice' to your shopping list or we'll be through all mine in no time!'

5

Jo felt her whole body deflate. The 'insensitive beast'! He'd done that deliberately! He knew she had been expecting him to kiss her. Well, more fool her. He wouldn't get another chance.

Harry was already striding at a steady pace through the soft muddy ground and Jo hastily fell into step at his side, wisely letting the incident drop. It was hot and steamy and they would need their breath and energy for the trek ahead of them.

By the time they came to a fork in the track darkness had fallen and the chatter of the rainforest creatures had long since ceased. Harry shone a torch on a wooden signpost and they were relieved to note that it pointed the way to the Orang-utan Centre. They had drunk all of their water and were feeling tired and they gratefully trudged in the direction it pointed.

A glimmer of light drew them towards their target — the dark silhouette of a wooden chalet-style building on stilts over a metre high. Harry reached it first and he climbed up the rough step-ladder calling out, 'Hello, there! Is anyone at home?'

The Malaysian man of about thirty and of stocky build who flung open the door seemed taken aback to see them on the small veranda.

'Harry Bretherton,' Harry introduced himself, holding out his hand. 'You expected me earlier, I think?'

The man recovered his poise. 'Ah, Mr Bretherton! Yes, yes! We wondered what happened to you. Welcome! Come in. You are very wet. Ah, and a young lady!'

His face looked dismayed as Jo appeared in view at the top of the steps.

'This is Jo Mattison, my photographer,' Harry introduced her.

'But, you too, are soaking wet!' He

peered outside into the darkness. 'Where have you parked your truck? I didn't hear it arrive. You did pick it up at the airport, didn't you?'

Harry laughed humourlessly. 'Yes . . . but, unfortunately, a tree fell on top of us a few miles back along the track. We've had to abandon it for the time being.'

'What? But how terrible! And you are both uninjured?'

'Thankfully, yes.'

The man drew them indoors into the wooden building. 'You must be tired and hungry. We have just eaten, but I will get Lip to fix something for you. He does a lot of the 'hands-on' work around here. He's just out the back. I'll give him a shout. My name is Sim Junara, by the way. I have been acting as the manager here since Mike's accident.'

Jo was gazing around the wooden interior of the simple building. The walls and windows of the sparsely-furnished small communal room were hung with raffia blinds and there were a few cupboards around its perimeter and some mats on the floor. A small alcove to one side seemed to serve as the kitchen and the smell of cooking hung in the air, making her aware of how hungry she was.

'We need to get out of these wet things,' she said to Harry. 'Where do you suppose our rooms will be? And the bathroom?'

'Ah!' The cautious exclamation came from Sim as he re-entered the room. 'The bathroom is a very simple affair round the back,' he explained, looking apologetic from Harry to Jo. 'I'm afraid the young lady will find it very primitive. We didn't expect you to bring a female with you, Mr Bretherton.'

'Just how simple?' Jo asked, uneasily prepared for the answer that came.

'As I said, a primitive affair typical of rural Borneo . . . some planks over a dug-out hole . . . but it has a canvas cover around it.'

'Great!' Jo murmured, with a sidelong

glance at Harry. His face was impassive
. . . but his left eyebrow was slightly
raised and she knew he was hoping she
wouldn't show ingratitude to their host.
She forced a smile.

'And for washing?'

'Yourself or your clothes?'

The question was asked blandly, but
Jo had a suspicion that the man was
enjoying the information he was giving
her.

'Both, I suppose.'

'We wash our clothes once a week in
the kitchen over there . . . but no
detergents, please . . . and, for our
bodies, we have rigged up a shower by a
small freshwater pool down the stream
a little way. We will show you the way
tomorrow. For tonight, it will be hands
and face only. Water is used sparingly as
it all has to be carried from the stream.
Lip will show you the collecting point.'

'And our sleeping quarters?' Harry
enquired.

'A simple bunk-house leads off
through the door over there. Space for a

number of mats on the floor,' Sim said, spreading his hands wide. 'The boys we get as workers here aren't used to sleeping in beds . . . and it leaves more of the money to go towards the cost of running this place.'

Jo didn't know whether to laugh hysterically or burst into tears. She felt so tired, her brain wasn't functioning properly and but for being so hungry, all she would like to do was to curl up on a mat anywhere. Instead she smiled again.

'That's fine. I'm used to camping. I'm sure I'll manage.'

She yawned widely and covered her mouth with her hand. 'Do excuse me.'

'I'll get Lip to rig up a curtain in the bunk-house,' Sim offered, 'then you can turn in as soon as you have eaten. Here, take this lamp through and you can choose your corner.'

Harry took hold of the oil-lamp that Sim unhooked from a bracket on the wall and Jo followed as he led the way, holding the lamp in front of him. Some rolled mats were stacked against a wall; a few articles of clothing were hanging from some wooden pegs on the wall.

This was home for the next few weeks!

It wasn't quite light when Jo awoke the following day and it took her a few moments to remember where she was. She groaned and turned over. According to her brain, it wasn't yet midnight of the previous day. It was 'sleep-time', not 'waking-up time'! But she could hear voices as Sim and Lip dressed themselves and left the room to go for their morning shower.

'Up you get, Jo!' Harry stirred her. 'I know you feel rough, but the sooner you adapt to the time zone the better. Just think how glad you'll be to drop onto your mat tonight!'

Jo groaned again. 'Don't talk about dropping onto a mat! It feels like I've slept on a pile of rocks!' She sat up and ran her fingers through her hair. 'I'm looking forward to that shower, though.'

She struggled to her feet, grabbed her

towel and toiletry bag and staggered after Harry. As she stepped onto the veranda though, she stopped in awe. The sky had lightened considerably in the past few minutes and there was a swathe of mist drifting among the trees of the rain forest, rising up through the treetops.

'It's beautiful, isn't it? Everywhere is so green and fresh-looking.'

The jungle creatures were wakening and she could hear the rasping chirp of the cicadas, the throaty calls of frogs and the sweeter sound of birds. Another sound that she couldn't identify seemed to bubble across the valley and as she turned questioningly in its direction, Harry supplied the answer.

'That's the call of the gibbons. They're probably over the hill in the next valley, but their sound carries in the clear air. Just like the sound of the stream. Listen! It's this way. Come on.'

They could hear voices as they scrambled down to the stream and met Sim and Lip head on as they reached a flat rocky area. After greeting each other, Harry asked them, 'Are we nearly there?'

'It's just around the next bend. We see you soon for breakfast, yes?'

'Yes. We won't be long.'

When they reached the gurgling stream Jo looked up into the overhanging trees for something that might feasibly be a substitute for a shower, a hosepipe threaded up through the branches, perhaps.

'It must be further on,' she suggested seeing nothing that resembled a shower.

Harry laughed as he parted the leaves of a bush at the water's edge. 'We're at the right spot', and indicating a metal colander that was suspended from a branch with a knotted rope, 'this seems to be the shower! There's a bucket here, as well. I guess we take it in turns to pour for each other! Do you want to go first, or shall I?'

'Well, you needn't think I'm going to take my clothes off and stand there whilst you pour water over me!' Jo

74

snapped in disappointment, seeing her longed-for shower receding fast.

'Just strip to your underwear. It will soon dry on you in this heat.' Harry suggested, unfeelingly grinning at her as she stood resolutely on the side of the stream, her hands on her hips, deflated by the lack of privacy and her doubts about the wisdom of coming out here after all.

'Why didn't you tell me it would be like this?' she pouted, knowing she sounded childish, but unable to restrain the question.

Harry shrugged. 'I didn't know. It's a bit more civilised at Sepilok where I was before. But I doubt if you would have taken much notice even if I had known. You were pretty desperate to get away. Changing your mind, are you? Where's your sense of adventure gone to?'

She shouldn't have come. She had acted far too impulsively and was now paying the price. If she were back at home she would be asleep in bed with the prospect of a nice warm shower in the privacy of her own bathroom to look forward to in the morning. And the possibility of Alec arriving any day to fulfil her dreams — not this freezing cold mountain stream to shock her into activity.

Harry watched her in exasperation. He knew exactly what she was thinking. She was having second thoughts about this whole escapade and was wishing she hadn't persuaded him to bring her — but he knew her doubts were aggravated by the disorientation of mind and body brought on by the eight hours difference in time-zone.

He wryly admitted that he was as much to blame as Jo was. He'd known it was a bad idea. He should have gone ahead without a photographer and arranged for one to follow out later. That would have been the sensible option . . . but when did sense have anything to do with his feelings for Jo?

He had always known it was Alec who was the lodestar of Jo's life. He should have let things go to their natural conclusion, even if it meant that Alec would seize his opportunity to become Willoughby's heir.

But that, he knew, was the reason why he had whisked Jo away. She deserved better than marriage without love . . . deserved, at least, the opportunity to step away from the situation and not run too hastily into it. Regretfully, he knew he had only delayed the inevitable. Alec wouldn't readily give up his hope to inherit Willoughby's fortune.

Still, Jo was here in Borneo and Alec wasn't! So, he slung his towel over a branch and proceeded to strip to his boxer shorts, saying briskly, 'I'll go first. You can pour.'

Jo watched as he stepped down into the stream. As he splashed some water over his bronzed skin, his muscles rippled with health and vitality . . . and Jo felt a spurt of admiration flaring deep within her.

'Come on! Get your shirt and shorts off and make yourself useful. Fill that bucket and pour it through the colander!'

Cajoled into activity, Jo pushed away her unnerving thoughts and quickly stripped off her outer clothes. She gasped with shock as she joined Harry in the stream, but swiftly plunged the bucket into the fast-flowing stream and scooped up some water.

'You've asked for it!' she warned as she tipped it into the colander, laughing in delight as Harry's involuntary shout as the cold water hit his skin and squealing when Harry's antics splashed the water at her. They laughed together as she scooped up more water and an inevitable water fight evolved. It was cold but invigorating and as Jo lifted up her face to the falling droplets, now exhilarating in its freshness, she felt more alert than she had since their arrival in Borneo.

Harry eventually hung the bucket on a branch of the tree.

'Enjoy that?' he asked, turning to face her.

He didn't mean to draw her into his arms, but it happened before he had time to stop himself . . . and she didn't immediately pull herself away, although she looked as surprised as he felt.

'Yes, I felt alive again,' she said breathlessly, her hands against his glistening chest. She could feel his heart thudding against her hands.

As she hesitated, Harry pulled her closer and placed his mouth firmly on hers.

Jo's heart leaped and somersaulted within her chest but, after a momentary, startled hesitation, she responded in kind, enjoying his kiss at a deeper level than she had ever known.

The pressure from Harry's lips relaxed slightly, but then was renewed in a more sensuous manner, making Jo's lips quiver under his velvet touch, demanding more.

Harry's hands were holding her close to him. She could feel the pounding of his heart and felt her own heart matching its rhythm. Her legs felt weak and as she relaxed against him, she imagined him picking her up in his arms and carrying her . . . carrying her . . .

6

Her imagination was racing ahead in tune with her senses and she felt powerless to intervene, powerless to pull away, powerless to do anything to break the tide that was sweeping them along — and it was Harry who brought the magical moment to an end. He lifted his lips from hers and they stared at each other in silent recognition of what had been happening.

Harry felt elated by Jo's response. He knew he hadn't imagined it. What had just happened between them had been a moment of revelation, a meeting of matched desire, a promise of what could be . . . and yet . . . ?

He felt Jo's body stiffen slightly and she drew back a little, holding out the palm of her hand towards him.

'No,' she whispered.

Harry sensed that she was puzzled by

what had transpired. She had returned the fervour of his passion . . . but had she truly known what she was doing?

So he didn't pull her back towards him, although he wanted to. He wanted to draw him against him and be moulded to her, flesh upon flesh. He wanted to kiss her again until she was hopelessly senseless as he felt . . . but he knew that 'senseless' was the right word . . .

. . . so, instead, he pulled his thoughts back to practicalities.

'Sorry! That was a bit stupid of me,' he apologised. He mentally shook his thoughts. 'I'll help you up the bank,' he said, letting go of her and taking hold of an overhanging branch of the tree. He hauled himself out of the stream. 'Up you come!'

Turning his back to her, Harry draped his towel around his hips whilst Jo vigorously rubbed at her legs to bring some life back to them and then dragged her damp shorts and T-shirt back on, her mind full of jumbled emotions.

He turned to lead the way back to the Centre and Jo followed, her mind almost numb with confusion. Why had Harry kissed her like that? Why had she responded? What did Harry think of her? The way he was now striding ahead, the answer was, 'not very much!'

She felt a surge of resentment. It was he who had initiated the kiss. Was this going to spoil their relationship as they worked together? She hoped not. She touched her lips gently with the tips of her fingers, recalling the sensation of Harry's kiss and felt confused. It was obvious that he was regretting kissing her already. She wondered again if she had made a mistake in coming here and sighed with the frustration of not knowing. Only time would tell.

In the meantime, there was a job to do and she had better follow Harry's lead and forget the incident had happened . . . which, although she felt awkward at first, she managed to do.

Breakfast was a simple affair of fruit

juice, fruit and muesli, not too different from what they later gave to the eight juvenile orang-utans in residence at the Centre, Jo reflected in amusement.

She was enchanted by the young creatures that Sim brought out of the overnight nursery comfortably nestling together in a wheelbarrow. He wheeled them inside the day-enclosure, fastening the door behind him.

Jo and Harry watched through the double layers of wire-meshed fencing as Sim encouraged them out of the wheelbarrow onto the series of looped ropes and hanging tyres that made a simple sort of exercise apparatus similar to an adventure playground for children in western parks.

The juveniles were about sixty centimetres tall, their bodies covered with long, straight coarse red hair. Their arms were long and gangly, their hands and feet relatively large . . . but it was their faces that captivated Jo.

'Oh, they're adorable!' she exclaimed, squatting down by the linked-wire wall.

One of the juveniles squatted opposite her and regarded her seriously, his head cocked to one side. 'Oh, just look at this one! I'm sure he thinks I am the one under inspection!'

Jo laughed. 'They're gorgeous! I can see why people are tempted to want one as a pet. They are so appealing. Can I come in and help to feed them?'

'Another day,' Sim advised. 'Let them get used to your presence here first.'

Lip arrived with a bucket containing various fresh fruits and another half-filled with a runny milk and cereal mix that reminded Jo of thin semolina. The young orang-utans immediately abandoned their play and ambled towards Lip, chattering loudly and with complete disregard for manners, dipped their paws and mouths into the glutinous mash.

Later, leaving Jo in Lip's care at the Centre, Sim took Harry on his small motorcycle back to where they had left the truck the previous day. Leaving Jo's suitcase to be picked up on their way back, they then travelled to Ranau, the nearest cluster of commercial buildings and houses, where Harry arranged to have the damaged truck collected and a replacement sent out from the hire firm in Kota Kinabalu.

He also telephoned his father whilst he was in range of a signal for his mobile phone. 'I carefully worked out what to say and didn't tell Dad that you were here with me,' Harry told Jo on his return, ' . . . but I thought your uncle might be worried out of his mind about you . . . and, in his present state of health, that wouldn't be very good for him.'

'Mmm, you're right,' Jo admitted. 'I have been concerned about him worrying about where I am. So, what did you say exactly?'

'Just that I had taken you where you asked me to and that you are safely there . . . and that you would get in touch in a couple of weeks or so when you didn't feel quite to upset about what he had done. OK?'

'Yes . . . and you managed to get my suitcase! Great!'

The hour or so spent apart seemed to have distanced them from the morning's lapse of self-control and now, with most of the morning gone, Harry decided that after a light meal of chicken and rice, they would make their first foray into the rainforest to see what was available in the way of food for the orang-utans.

Glad to be doing the job she had come to do, Jo enthusiastically took photographs as Harry noted various fruit trees . . . the yellow fleshy mangoes; wild fig trees; red-plum-size fruits called rambutans; banana trees and durians, a fruit with an appalling smell but a taste as smooth and sweet as custard. All of which were good indications that the area of forest was capable of sustaining their rehabilitation programme.

Jo was relieved that they had both returned to their former relationship. She had obviously read too much into

Harry's kiss, she reflected in self-chastisement. It had been a momentary lapse . . . not to be repeated, she sternly told herself.

Thankfully, Harry seemed to have arrived at the same conclusion and Jo found herself relaxing in his company again. She truly valued their friendship and didn't want to jeopardise it.

They had travelled for about half-an-hour, when the sound of a series of quiet bubbling grunts filtered through the forest. Even as Harry lightly touched Jo's arm to draw her attention to it, the sound built up into a full-blown gravelly roar that reverberated through the treetops.

'That's the call of a male orang-utan,' he whispered, 'and it's heading this way. It will be the dominant male of this section of the forest.'

'How do you know?'

'Only the dominant male develops the large cheek sacs that enable him to make the noise. Take the dominant male away and another male will develop the cheek flanges.'

Harry once more laid his hand on Jo's arm as the trees in the far distance had begun to shake. 'Look! He's coming! Get your camera ready!'

Jo did so, selecting 'multi burst' mode on the camera settings and held her breath as the trees shook more and more vigorously. Within seconds, the awesome sight of a one-and-a-half metre tall, orange-haired creature swung lazily into view, his long arms languorously reaching out in alternate motion to the branches and creepers of the rainforest's canopy.

Harry touched her arm, placed a finger to his lips to discourage her speaking and then gestured his hand in an arc to indicate that the orang-utan was heading away from them.

'Come on. Let's follow,' Harry whispered. 'Quietly, now!'

Jo reflected that, with the crashing of branches marking his progress, there wasn't much danger of the orang-utan hearing their stealthy progress along the forest floor.

'Why are we following him? What's he going to do?'

'Hopefully, I think he might be looking for a suitable place to build a nest for his afternoon sleep. See, there he goes, up to the fork of those branches. See how he's twisting the branches under him.'

Jo recorded the activity on her camera in awed silence, her heart racing with excitement, feeling privileged at being so close to this magnificent creature. A series of low grunts and gentle shaking of the fragile construction indicated that the orang-utan was comfortably settling himself and when they shortly heard a gentle snore Harry and Jo grinned at each other.

Over the next few days, they trekked through the rainforest counting yet more fruit trees and nests, estimating the forest's ability to support its inhabitants and occasionally, sighting the elusive creatures, always singly, unless it were a female with her latest off-spring clinging to her chest, peeping out through the curtain of coarse red hair.

Jo found the work and the unhurried life-style to be both soothing and stimulating at the same time. Their venture had purpose and great satisfaction was felt as Harry's recorded figures built up to show that the area was suitable for the Centre's presence and purpose and they knew it would, almost certainly, be approved by the local authority.

Surprisingly, Sim wasn't so sure. 'There are too many resident orang-utans in the area,' he argued. 'I think we should leave this area to manage itself. If we interfere too much and relocate juveniles here from other areas, over a prolonged period of time there will not be enough food for them.'

'Yes, there will,' Harry disagreed. 'The area is very rich in fruit and besides the fruit, there are leaves, twigs, bark, honey and animal foods such as termites, ants, bees, birds' eggs and small lizards. From what I've seen it's an ideal area. I know Mike thought so, too.'

'Mike saw only what he wanted to see!' Sim stated firmly. 'You ask around what local farmers and plantation owners think. You will hear a different story, I think.'

7

No matter what Harry said about the abundance of food in the forest, Sim would not back down and the atmosphere was a bit tense that evening. Fortunately, the following day was the date given by the truck-hire firm for Harry's replacement truck to be available for collection from Ranau.

Leaving Jo at the centre with Lip, Harry once more rode pillion behind Sim.

'Will you plug my mobile phone in on the way back, to recharge its battery?' Jo asked. 'I know we can't get a signal here, but we may move into areas that are within range once we can get about more. It feels strange not to be in contact with people.'

Harry wondered if the general term 'people' really meant Alec . . . but knew there was nothing he could do about it and agreed to her request.

'What will you do whilst I'm gone?' he asked her. 'I'll be away about three to four hours, I should think.'

'I think I'll transfer more of my photographs onto my laptop. I've still got a good hour of battery-life left, so I should get quite a few viewed and edited. I'll need to recharge that battery as well once we have the truck.'

The sound of the low-powered engine puttered gradually away and Jo decided to watch Lip going through the morning routine with the juvenile orang-utans. One of the youngsters had been found near the fallen body of his mother. Tom, Marlon and Jacob, three males and Ayako, Judi, Babi and Kiri, females, had been rescued from being held as illegal pets and were used to being with humans.

The main task was to wean them off the support and Tom, the eldest, was already being taken for short journeys into the rainforest each day and was being shown a variety of fruit trees that would provide him with a suitable diet. The past few days, Harry had started to feed him only bananas at the centre to encourage him to forage for a more varied diet in the forest and he plucked his fill from these trees . . . but always leaped back onto Harry's shoulder when he turned to walk away.

Jo knew they would miss him when he finally left them, but his departure would mean the centre's job had been well done.

She left Lip putting them through their paces on the climbing ropes and was soon engrossed in downloading some of the many photographs she had taken. Jo was laughing at a picture of Ayako hanging from the rope by one hand and her two feet, her legs bent up behind her back, holding the rope above her shoulders and eating a banana held in her other hand, when she heard the gentle phut-phut of a motorbike.

She glanced at her watch. Surely Sim wasn't back so soon? Something must have gone wrong with the arrangements.

But as the sound of voices drifted up to her, she knew it wasn't Sim's voice she could hear. Since she had seen no visitors at all since their arrival, she leaned forward and looked curiously through the open side to see who it was. The voices were speaking in the Malay language, but she could tell from the tone that the visitor was expressing himself with some agitation and anxiety, with Lip responding in like manner.

Jo left her seat and went to the doorway. 'Is something wrong, Lip?' she called down to him.

Both men glanced up to her. The stranger looked from Jo back to Lip and passed a light comment, but Lip didn't respond with levity.

'You come here, Miss Jo,' he requested.

Jo ran lightly down the steps. 'What's the matter?'

'This man say that a female orang-utan has been injured on the plantation where he works. The manager wants to kill it, but some of the workers said it would not be right.

'Too right, it wouldn't!' Jo agreed, smiling encouragingly at the man. 'Is it far away?'

'Only a few miles,' Lip assured her. 'He says you go with him and speak to the manager then he will not do this wrong thing!'

'Me?' Jo squeaked. 'Why me? I can't speak Malay.'

'No, but the manager he speak English. He take notice of you, Miss Jo . . . but not me. I am just *boy*.'

Yes, Jo could see the reasoning in that. Well, if it took an indignant English girl to persuade the manager that his workers were right, then so be it.

She disappeared back inside, switched off her laptop and grabbed hold of her day-pack, glad that she had refilled the water bottle with purified water earlier in anticipation of needing it later.

The man was astride his motorbike waiting for her and she lost no time in slipping her arms through the bag's straps, hitching it onto her back and taking the seat behind him. Her feet were barely off the ground when the rider twisted the clutch-grip, slipped into gear — and they were off, dirt from the track scattered far and wide behind them.

'Tell Harry where I've gone!' Jo yelled back to Lip, not knowing from the wave of his arm whether or not he had heard her.

They were soon back on the main track through the forest. Jo tried to keep her bearings of where they were in relation to the centre but, after making a number of turns at T-junctions and forks in the track, she knew she was well and truly disorientated. She wasn't aware of another motor scooter approaching until they had almost met.

Her driver fractionally slowed down, but then simply swerved to one side and they passed each other a little too closely for Jo's peace of mind. As she glanced back over her shoulder, she frowned. Surely that was a young orang-utan's head she could see sticking out of the knapsack on the motorcyclist's back?

She tapped the driver urgently on his shoulder. 'Stop!'

He slammed on the brakes and Jo lurched forward into his back. 'What the matter, miss?'

'That man! He had a young orang-utan in the bag on his back! What's he doing with it?'

The young man shrugged. 'I not know. Maybe he take it to your centre?'

'Ah! Yes, that could be possible. Yes, OK. I didn't think of that!'

She lifted up her feet and they were off again. Not much further on she could see that the rainforest was thinning out ahead of them and when they reached the next T-junction, the area ahead was planted with palm trees, mature ones to the right and young trees to the left. They turned left and drove up the track between the edge of the rainforest to the left and the palm plantation to the right. After about ten minutes, Jo could see a small group of men ahead.

A man, in his mid-thirties she reckoned, stood slightly apart from a group of older men and Jo guessed that he was the manager. As Jo dismounted from her pillion seat, the man spoke in rapid sentences to her driver. The only word Jo could identify was 'Sim'.

Her driver shook his head and replied in his natural tongue, pointing with his hand towards Jo. Whatever it was that he was saying, it did nothing to appease the manager, who didn't look pleased to see her. Pleased or not, Jo knew she had to take control of the situation. Not wanting to undermine his position of authority unless he proved awkward, she held out her hand, smiling encouragingly.

'Good day. My name is Jo Mattison. I work at the Rehabilitation Centre. You have a problem, I believe.'

The man briefly took her hand. 'Yes, miss. I am Navin Joshi. I represent Mr

Chennaiyah, the owner of this plantation, but he is away at present and so I must make decisions in his place. These man are in my control, but they are being very obstinate and refuse to allow me to dispose of the injured orang-utan. I know Mr Chennaiyah will be very angry. He does not want orang-utans on his plantation. They destroy his trees and make him lose profit. You understand? Yes?'

'Yes, I understand,' Jo replied, 'but it is against the law to kill orang-utans. They are a protected species. Where is the injured female?'

The man pointed to the group of men and as Jo approached them, they made way for her to pass between them to where she could see the wounded creature lying on the ground. She was entangled in a large net that had been thrown over her to restrain her attempts to escape into the forest. Jo went over to her and could see that, by her right shoulder, the ground was stained dark red.

'How was she injured?'

'Mr Chennaiyah say I must shoot any orang-utans I see destroying his trees. All those trees over there were damaged last night. I only obey my boss.'

Jo dropped to her knees beside the orang-utan, jumping back a little when the animal bared her teeth and snarled.

'It's all right! It's all right! I won't hurt you,' she said in a soothing voice, hoping the creature would somehow know that she was friend not foe. Not daring to even touch the prone creature, Jo felt extremely inadequate and at a loss how to proceed . . . but she knew she must demand safety for the orang-utan, whatever else she felt lacking.

As she straightened up, one of the men spoke. 'It is bad luck to kill orang-utan, miss.'

'That is superstitious folklore!' the young manager countered, looking at Jo for approval. 'Mr Chennaiyah must protect his property.'

'It may be so,' Jo agreed, 'but he has

done nothing to protect his border. This orang-utan knows nothing about plantation owners' rights. She, or certainly her ancestors, will have roamed through this area since time began. How is she to know that these tasty trees are not for her to eat?'

'Exactly!' Mr Joshi agreed, pouncing on what he saw as a point in his boss's favour. 'So, we kill them to keep them out.'

As a growl of disapproval ran through the crowd, Jo countered swiftly, 'No! Mr Chennaiyah must put a protective fence around his land!'

'That would cost too much! It is not worth it!'

'It is the only way! I will send MY boss around to speak to him . . . but for now, we must decide what to do for this poor creature. I can't treat her here. We need to get her to the Centre. Have you got a truck?'

'Mr Chennaiyah will not like it! And you men get back to your work!' he shouted impatiently to the crowd of workers.

'Mr Chennaiyah will have to put up with it! Look, Mr Joshi,' she drew him aside. 'Your men are getting restless about all this delay. I appreciate that you're in a tight spot in all this, but your men have the law on their side. If you want to keep control of them, I suggest you begin to co-operate . . . and start by bringing an open-backed truck around here. We'll take the orangutan to the Centre and see what we can do for her.'

Seeing the sense in what she was saying, Mr Joshi strode off down the track, hopefully, Jo thought, to bring back a suitable truck. She turned to the group of men.

'Now, you men, will you be able to carefully lift her into the truck Mr Joshi is going to bring? You'll have to be very gentle with her.'

A hand touched her shoulder and Jo looked up into the man's face. It was one of the group of workers.

'Orang-utan have little one,' he said.

'Ah, yes!' Jo remembered the juvenile

in the motorcyclist's knapsack. 'Has it been taken to the Centre?'

The man shrugged. 'I know nothing,' he said, looking over his shoulder a little furtively. 'I just tell you.'

Jo frowned, sending more to this. 'Who took it?'

'I not know.'

Jo took up the information with Mr Joshi when he returned with a truck, but he adamantly refused to admit any knowledge of a juvenile and when Jo asked him to question his workers, he again refused.

They progressed slowly. As they approached the Centre, Jo caught a glimpse of the tailend of a motorbike disappearing in the opposite direction. Was it Sim? She wasn't sure. She could have done with his help . . . but they would have to manage without him.

A glance at the parking space showed that Harry had not yet returned but, between them, Lip and the men who had accompanied Jo in the truck carefully unloaded the female orang-utan and carried her in the net into one of the rooms in the night enclosure.

'Where did you put the new juvenile, Lip?' Jo asked as the men took their leave.

Was it her imagination or did his eyes betray a sign of alarm as she shook his head vigorously.

'No new juvenile, Miss Jo.'

'There must be! I saw it being brought here.'

'No, miss. You mistaken! No-one brought new juvenile here.'

What was the use? Lip had said no new juvenile had been brought and he wasn't going to change his answer. She felt a wave of suspicion flood her mind.

'Where has Sim gone to?' she asked sharply.

Again Lip seemed alarmed by her question. 'Er, Sim take Mr Harry . . . ' he began, but paused with relief filling his eyes when the sound of a motorbike was heard.

Jo's first hope was that this was the courier with the juvenile but, as she hurried round to the front, she saw Sim parking his motorbike in the parking area.

He looked up as Jo hurried forward, closely followed by Lip. His gaze flitted to Lip and back to Jo. 'Is something the matter?'

'Yes. We have an injured female orang-utan and her youngster seems to have gone missing.'

Sim again glanced at Lip and Lip began to speak swiftly in Malay. Sim frowned at him.

'In English, please!' Jo snapped.

Lip haltingly explained the situation to Sim.

Sim shrugged. 'These plantation workers cannot be trusted. They probably want to make things difficult for Mr Chennaiyah. If a juvenile has been taken anywhere, it is either out of the district by now or being kept hidden somewhere. We shall probably hear no more about it unless the rangers pick up on it.' He shrugged again, smiling apologetically to Jo. 'We cannot save them all.'

'But I saw it being brought in this direction,' Jo insisted. 'And I saw you leaving as I returned with the injured female. Where have you been?'

Sim spread his hands wide. 'I have only just returned from taking Harry to Ranau,' he said, his face bland. 'I assure you, Miss Jo, you are mistaken if you think you saw me leaving. What are you accusing me of?'

Jo bit her lower lip. She couldn't be totally sure she had positively identified Sim. 'I'm not accusing you of anything, Sim. I just feel all is not right here . . . and we need to take it further.'

'I will contact the rangers,' Sim offered. 'Now, let me have a look at this injured female.'

When Harry arrived back with the replacement rental truck, Jo related the incident to him, expressing her concern about the missing juvenile.

Harry nodded. 'It could be a stealing,' he agreed, as he went to examine the sedated female. 'We'll let the rangers know tomorrow . . . but, right now, I'm more concerned about the mother. She's lost a lot of blood. All we can do is keep her comfortable and see how she is in the morning. By the way,' he added, 'your mobile phone is charged up.'

He slipped hand into his hip pocket and handed the phone to her. 'I heard a message come into it whilst I was within range of a signal.'

'Oh? Who's it from?'

She pressed the appropriate pads to unlock the keyboard and read the message. The name at the top of the small screen caused her to draw in her breath. It was Alec's.

Hav been looking 4 u. No success. Where r u? Urgent I c u. X Alec.

8

The following day, after the morning routine at the Centre had been completed, Harry examined the injured female, whom Jo had christened Annie, after the title character of one of her favourite childhood stories. He wasn't happy with her progress.

'I think it will be best for Annie if we take her to Sepilok. She'll stand a better chance there. They've got better facilities and their vet has had more experience than I have. The bullet went straight through her, but she has lost a lot of blood. If you take Tom into the rainforest with Lip, I'll drive towards the plantation and try to get a phone signal so that I can phone Sepilok to see if they can take her.

'What if her youngster turns up?' Jo wanted to know.

'We'll reunite them, of course.'

He didn't add that he held very little hope of the youngster being found. Jo had shared her misgivings about the events of the previous afternoon and although he was sceptical about any involvement by Sim in the affair, he was ready to believe that the youngster had been removed from the area and was probably far away by now.

Once he had left, Jo and Lip took Tom into the forest to hunt for fruit trees and they were pleased with the way he used his initiative. They found wild figs, mangoes and bananas and at one point Tom climbed up into a tree and swung himself out of sight.

When Lip turned to return to the Centre, Jo protested that they must wait for Tom. She knew that their ultimate aim was for the orang-utans to return to the forest to live independent lives, but she didn't feel Tom was ready yet. He enjoyed the company of the other juveniles too much for that.

'He will come if he wants to,' Lip said calmly.

Reluctantly, Jo followed him, looking anxiously over her shoulder.

They hadn't taken many steps when they heard a gentle crashing in the trees to their right and the leaves began to shake. A few moments later, a hair red arm parted the foliage and Tom's huge brown eyes stared down at them. He made noisy kissing sounds and chattered crossly at them.

Jo laughed delightedly. 'He's coming!'

'Yes, he not ready to leave us yet,' Lip agreed.

Harry had already returned. 'I phoned the rehabilitation centre at Sepilok to put them in the picture regarding Annie. They agree that she will have a better chance of recovery if we take her there, Jo. They're quite a few years ahead of us there and it will give you an idea of where we hope to take this project.'

After satisfying himself that Annie, if not showing signs of getting better, was at least stable, Harry took Lip with him on another investigative trip into another area of the rainforest, leaving Jo and Sim at the centre. Jo took the opportunity to take more photographs of the antics of the four resident juveniles and a few sensitive shots of Annie, while Sim prepared the fruit for the next feeding time and then prepared their own meal.

The sound of an unknown Malaysian voice drifted through the open-sided walls of the dwelling and Jo recognised Sim's voice in reply. Later, when she asked who had called, it said it was one of the rangers who had called for any up-to-date information on the injured female.

'I told him she is to be taken to Sepilok tomorrow.'

'Didn't he want to speak to me about the missing youngster?' Jo asked.

Sim shrugged. 'They have talked to the men at the plantation and are making their own enquiries elsewhere. If the juvenile has been stolen, the trail will be cold by now. We win some . . . we lose some.'

Jo held niggling doubts as to his sincerity, but didn't have sure enough grounds to voice them. When Harry returned, he was pleased to announce that they had found more evidence of the area's abundant fruit trees and he was confident that the Centre was in the right place.

'So, tomorrow, Jo and I will be off to Sepilok,' he announced at suppertime. 'I'll leave you in charge, Sim and Lip can take Tom into the forest for his morning foraging trip. Is that OK with you two?'

Sim and Lip agreed and as soon as Harry and Jo had eaten an early breakfast the following day, they carefully manoeuvred the sedated Annie into the back of the truck, made sure she was comfortable and set out on their journey.

After the resident vet had examined Annie and overseen her transfer to the hospital wing. Harry gave Jo a conducted tour. Learning that it was almost time for the regular morning feeding session, they followed other visitors along a wooden walkway into the rainforest until they came within sight of the elevated feeding stations.

'This is what we need to do at our centre,' Harry told her. 'See, we're away from the actual centre, so the rehabilitated orang-utans can live in the rainforest, but come back here to feed in their early days of independence . . . and of course, the staff can keep an eye on them.'

'Won't the orang-utans take the easier option and just keep in the habit of coming here to feed?' Jo queried.

'No, they just provide bananas and a thickened milk drink here. It will ward off starvation without being too attractive as a main diet.'

When Harry left her for a short while to talk over what he was doing at their own centre with the senior warden at Sepilok, Jo took out her mobile phone and accessed Alec's message again, undecided what to do about it.

She had let go of her initial anger at

Uncle Willoughby's ridiculous plan to settle his inheritance on whichever cousin she married, and now that she was safely distanced from the situation, she felt it would be childish to continue to keep her whereabouts a secret. After Alec's show of concern for her, she also felt she owed it to him to let him know where she was and that she was OK. It would keep the lines of communication open between them and on her return to England, she could meet up with him somewhere and see what might develop.

Accordingly, she quickly tapped out a return message and hoping she wouldn't later regret it, she selected *send*.

She now had a month or so to let it rest and in the meantime, she could concentrate on the photographic project she was doing with Harry.

Harry returned from his chat with the senior warden, highly enthused by the provision of building materials to make a wooden feeding station and a few hefty coils of rope, all of which more or less filled the back of the truck.

After they left the rehabilitation centre, they drove into Sandakan to replenish their grocery supplies and Harry suggested they treat themselves to a meal on the way back. Enjoying their brief respite from the simple life at the centre, Jo agreed and they found a delightful restaurant on the outskirts of the town. Seated opposite Harry in a secluded corner, Jo felt happy and relaxed and glancing across at Harry, it was obvious that he felt the same. He really was her dearest friend, she silently acknowledged.

Jo enjoyed the meal, but the wine made her feel slightly light-headed and when Harry took hold of her hand, gently stroking his thumb over the backs of her fingers, she was aware of a warm glow spiralling through her, jolting her out of the sense of ease. She didn't used to feel romantically attracted to him. Now, he was forever pulling her up short destroying her piece of mind . . . disturbing her complacency . . . activating a sense of anticipation deep within her.

Their eyes met and held and Jo's lips tingled with expectancy. She felt as though a magnetic force was drawing her to lean forward across the small table. She knew she wanted Harry to kiss her . . . but she had just returned a reply to Alec's text message. She shouldn't want to kiss Harry like this!

Her tumbling thoughts confused her and before she could stop herself, she pulled her hand away and blurted out, 'I've told Alec where I am.'

Jo saw a faint wry expression flicker across Harry's face and wished she hadn't spoken it out like that. She should have told him straightaway, not like this, spoiling the lovely evening they were having together.

'I thought you might,' Harry said quietly. 'What do you think Alec will do?'

'Nothing! What is there for him to do . . . except wait until I go home?'

Harry shrugged his shoulders. 'Depends how desperate he is!'

'Desperate?' Jo repeated, with an icy edge to her voice.

'Perhaps I should have said, 'keen',' Harry mollified.

Jo wished he hadn't said that, because she didn't truly expect Alec to do anything impulsive — and now, when he lived up to her low expectation, it would appear to Harry that Alec wasn't as much in love with her as she had tried to convince him . . . and herself.

'Alec is far too responsible a person to drop everything at a moment's notice and chase halfway around the world,' she said primly.

The congenial ambiance of their stolen hours away from the centre had cooled dramatically in the past few minutes and feeling uncomfortable at being the one to have caused the cooling, Jo finished her glass of wine, dabbed her lips with her napkin and stood up, pushing back her chair.

'Talking of which, I think we had better be on our way back, don't you?'

The air remained frosty for the first few miles of the journey home, but their friendship had stood too long to allow it to remain so and they were once more relaxed in their habitual friendship by the time Harry drove into his parking space at the centre.

Knowing that both Sim and Lip would be busy settling the juveniles down for the night, they went straight round to the rear of the small compound to let the two men know they had returned and to pass on the details of Annie's transfer to Sepilok. Something about Lip's demeanour alerted them to the fact that something was wrong as soon as they saw him.

He responded to their greeting, but continued to sweep out the day-nursery with his head down, refusing to make eye contact. Even Sim seemed a little discomfited.

'What's wrong?' Harry asked, glancing around. 'Is everyone safely tucked away for the night?'

'Not quite,' Sim admitted. 'When Lip

took Tom for his forage into the forest this afternoon, he didn't come back. He waited around but eventually gave up and came back without him. That's right, isn't it?'

9

'Yes,' Lip agreed, his eyes unhappy. 'I called his name and waited, but there was no sight nor sound of him. I hope he is all right.'

'Oh, dear,' Jo sympathised. 'We knew it was going to happen some day, didn't we?' She looked appealingly to Harry.

Harry's mouth twisted wryly. 'Yes, but I didn't think it would be so soon. I didn't think he was ready yet. Still, that is our eventual aim, so we mustn't get too disheartened by it, and you never know, Lip, he might be waiting out here for us in the morning.'

He was speaking more optimistically than he really felt because another reason for Tom's non-appearance might be that he had somehow injured himself in the forest. Occasionally, branches snapped under the sudden weight of an orang-utan and the luckless creature would fall to the ground — but that happened more often to older, larger orang-utans, not small juveniles.

'So don't be so downcast, Lip . . . and, if he doesn't make an appearance by tomorrow's feeding time, we'll organise a search for him. That's all we can do. It's part of the job, I'm afraid.'

Lip seemed grateful for the reassurance, but didn't appear to be much cheered. A sharp word from Sim caused his eyes to harden as he glanced at the older man and, at another snapped sentence, he silently leaned his broom against the outside wall and disconsolately trailed his way over to the living quarters.

'What did you say to him?' Harry asked.

Sim shrugged. 'I told him it was no use working here if he couldn't act like a man . . . and to make himself useful by cooking our meal.'

'Don't be too hard on him,' Harry advised. 'We all get attached to the juveniles.'

There was no sign of Tom the following day and, as promised, they went into the rainforest to make a search. Since Harry had decided to make an immediate start on building a feeding platform, they carried with them as much of the materials as they could carry to a small clearing Harry had already ear-marked as a suitable place.

They had to give up after a couple of hours as there was the daily routine at the centre to keep running and the feeding station to build. Sim was the obvious one to help Harry with the construction, so Jo and Lip returned to the centre, leaving the two men hard at work.

Jo spent some time helping Lip, enjoying the contact she was now allowed with the young orang-utans. They were like babies and young children and their antics on the ropes and climbing equipment caused much merriment.

It had been decided that Jo would

take some lunch to Harry and Sim, allowing them maximum construction time, in the hope that its swift construction would give Tom a point of contact with them if he were still in the area and, accordingly, she prepared the food and packed it into her back-pack, taking a good supply of drinking water.

On her return to the centre she saw a van parked there and could hear raised voices coming from the rear of the compound and, on investigation, she found Lip arguing with another man outside the day-nursery. The man was swarthy, middle-aged and seemed to be demanding something of Lip and had raised his arm in a threatening gesture.

'What's going on?' she asked sharply, taking an instant dislike to the stranger.

The man said something in his native tongue to Lip, causing Lip to step back hastily. Lip made some reply, shaking his head determinedly and indicating Jo with his hand. The man followed his gaze, snarled a reply and, turning abruptly, he stalked off to his van and drove away.

'What was all that about, Lip?' Jo demanded.

'He . . . he wanted work,' Lip said with some reluctance, ' . . . but I told him no work here for such as him.'

Somehow Jo wasn't entirely sure that she believed he was speaking the truth. There was something furtive about Lip's demeanour, something reminiscent of his manner the previous day that made her doubt him.

'What sort of work? Do you know him?'

'I have . . . seen him before — but he's a bad man!' Lip said, but then bit his lower lip as if regretting his words.

Jo was thankful when Harry and Sim returned to the Centre before darkness fell. She was aware of Lip's unease as she recounted the incident to them . . . and was also aware of what seemed to be warning glances directed at him by Sim. Lip added nothing to what he had already told Jo and Sim disclaimed any knowledge of the man . . . too quickly disclaiming, Jo thought, considering he had only been given a sketchy description of the man.

When they were alone, Harry asked, 'Did the man make you feel that you might be in danger here?'

Jo hesitated, 'Not so much in danger,' she said, weighing her words carefully, not wanting to unnecessarily cause alarm where none was warranted, ' . . . just uneasy. His anger seemed vented towards Lip more than towards me. I got the feeling that there was more to it than simply being denied an opportunity to work. He seemed to be refusing whatever was being asked of him more vehemently than a refusal of work would justify. There was anger . . . and fear . . . on his face.'

Harry was clearly perturbed by the incident. 'I think we had better stick closely together over the next few days,' he suggested. 'I don't want you to be here on your own in-case the man comes back.'

'I would be more anxious about leaving Lip on his own,' Jo pointed out. 'The man went soon after I made an appearance. I don't think he would have left so readily if I hadn't come back.'

'If you're right about Lip knowing more than he's letting on, that's his responsibility. You're mine!' Harry said firmly. 'If there's any likelihood of trouble, I think I would feel happier if you cut short your stay here and return to England. You've taken lots of photographs, haven't you?'

Jo felt a stab of cold steel slice into her. Leave? Leave the orang-utans? Leave Harry? She wasn't ready to leave yet; certainly not before the project was well in hand.

'Yes, but I want to see this phase of the scheme taken further,' she prevaricated. 'What danger could there possibly be, anyway? No, it was just some sort of argument between Lip and that man. Like he said, the man wanted work and Lip couldn't give him any.'

128

'Hmm, I'm not too sure,' Harry demurred. But, having no other information about the affair, he felt disinclined to make too big an issue of it. 'We'll see how it goes,' he temporised.

The following day Harry and Sim returned to the forest to finish the construction of the feeding station, reminding Jo that she had a whistle in her backpack. 'Use it if you want me to return,' he told her. 'I'm sure I'll hear it . . . and we'll come back for lunch then you don't have to leave Lip on his own.'

Jo spent some time with the juvenile orang-utans, trying to win Lip's confidence to confide in her by working alongside him and chatting pleasantly. However, he seemed disinclined to respond and eventually, she went indoors to work on her laptop.

The morning sped by and when Harry and Sim returned it was with the unwelcome news that the fruit they had left there the previous day was untouched . . . and the good news that the feeding station was fully erected and ready for the system of ropes to be added. Harry thought Lip would be the better one to help with that as he was of lighter weight and more agile than Sim . . . and, having no qualms at leaving the older man on his own, he suggested that Jo went with them after lunch, to photograph the finished work.

Harry had already chosen what he considered to be the most suitable trees to form part of the link-way and Lip had no problem in climbing up to test the strength of the trunks, marking the ones to be used. The rope they were to use was heavy and so Lip climbed the trees with a finer rope fastened around his waist, hauling up the heavier rope once he was straddled across a suitable branch about six metres above the ground.

Harry followed him up and, with Jo adding advice from ground level, they managed to make a double loop of rope around the tree trunks, fastening it securely with a series of hitched knots.

As they emerged from the trees, they

could see that one of the park rangers was there, talking to Sim beside his parked patrol truck. Something in Sim's stance indicated that he was ill at ease. When the ranger saw Harry, he left Sim and strode forward to greet him.

'Are you Mike Rowlinson's replacement?' he asked after bidding him good-day.

'Yes. My name's Harry Bretherton and this is my colleague, Jo Mattison. What can I do for you?'

The man glanced over his shoulder to where Sim was standing scowling at them and then over to Lip, who Harry and Jo now realised, had hardly moved since they had spotted the patrol vehicle.

'We've had a report that a number of young orang-utans have been offered for sale on the illegal market and the name of this place has been mentioned as a possible source of trade,' the man explained.

'Mr Junara naturally denies any knowledge of this matter, but our

131

informant mentioned his name during questioning. I hoped that Mr Junara would be willing to accompany me to Head Office so that we can discuss the matter, but he denies any involvement and says that you will vouch for him. Is that so?'

'I can vouch for him insofar as I've had no reason to suspect that he is part of this trade.' Harry told the ranger, reluctant to speak against a colleague without any specific charge or proof. 'As you know, I've only been here a short while . . . and Mike would be able to give him a better reference than I can.'

'Has any of your stock gone missing? There was mention of a recent transaction.'

A swift intake of Jo's breath caused the ranger to switch his attention to her.

'Yes?' he asked her.

After a slight hesitation, Jo said, 'A juvenile failed to return from a rehabilitation training trip in the rainforest the other day. We can't actually say he has gone missing, but we haven't sighted him since then. But, surely . . . ?'

She swung around to look at Lip, who was too far away to hear what they were saying, but seemed decidedly uncomfortable. Jo liked the lad, but there was no doubt that he felt guilty about something. However, this was a serious charge and she shared Harry's reluctance to be the one to cause upheaval in the lives of people they were working with.

'There's another juvenile who is possibly missing,' Harry intervened, deliberately taking the attention from Jo. 'There was an incident at one of the nearby palm oil plantations the other day. We took an injured female to Sepilok two days ago. She was reported to have a youngster with her, but we couldn't find it. Might that be the one in question?'

'That one has been mentioned to us as well,' the ranger agreed. 'We have heard of three definite sales in total. This trade has to be stopped immediately!'

'I couldn't agree more,' Harry affirmed. 'Each one they get away with gives them cause to trade again. And each successful trade usually leaves as many as half a dozen dead orang-utans along the trail. I just have no grounds to support the accusations against Sim. All I can say is that we'll keep a vigilant eye open for anything untoward happening.'

'There was the man yesterday,' Jo remembered, relating the rest if the incident to the ranger. 'But Lip gave him no encouragement. Maybe it's spite about that that has brought Sim's name into the problem? You know? 'You sent us away empty-handed, so now we'll drop you in it!' That sort of thing?'

The ranger pursed his lips, giving consideration to the thought. 'Maybe,' he agreed. He flicked his glance over the two Malaysian workers, then back to Harry. 'Here's my contact number,' handing Harry a small card. 'Keep your eyes open and let me know if you notice anything to support the verbal accusation.'

The following morning, when they awoke to find themselves left alone at the centre . . . with Sim, Lip and the motorbike missing, it seemed like their trouble had doubled.

10

'At least the orag-utans are safe!' Jo said in great relief when they had hurried round to the night-nursery to check on their inmates.

'Yes. Probably only thanks to this extra lock I put on the door last night,' Harry agreed. 'I wanted to be sure of their safety . . . and it seems I wasn't being over-cautious! And the fact I slept with the keys to our truck under my bed-roll!'

'Do you really think Sim and Lip have gone because they're guilty?' Jo asked pensively. 'It couldn't just be that they thought they might be unjustly blamed?'

Harry made a wry grimace. 'I doubt it. I told them last night that they had nothing to worry about if they were innocent of the charges . . . and Lip especially has been acting as though he had the weight of guilt on his shoulders.' He spread his hands in a helpless gesture. 'No. I'd say they've run before more substantial charges could be made against them.'

'I am disappointed though,' Jo said sadly. 'It's always worse when you are let down by people you know. And how are we going to manage the Centre on our own? I'm not really qualified to be in sole charge of the juveniles and you need to be able to get out and about to do your surveying of the forest.'

'I'll have to get in touch with Sepilok,' Harry decided. 'I'm sure they'll send out some extra help to tide us over . . . and I need to contact our ranger friend to let him know about Sim and Lip's defection. The sooner the better,' he added, glancing at his watch. 'I'm not happy about leaving you here alone, but one of us has to get within range of a mobile-phone satellite. If we get the juveniles safely locked into the day-nursery, you'll be able to manage their feeding programme and morning activity routine, won't you?'

'Sure!' Jo agreed.

After Harry had gone to make the phone-call, Jo got on with the morning routine feeling a mixture of anger, disappointment and a lingering shocked disbelief that Sim and Lip had been involved in the illegal sales of young orang-utans. How could they? The duplicity of it! Pretending to care for the juveniles whilst all the while setting up the sale of them!

Thoughts of Tom being taken into captivity were the most hurtful. He had learned how to survive in the forest; he had tasted freedom; he had been almost ready to live independently. The best she could hope for him would be that he was destined for a zoo . . . but with his familiarity with humans, he would fetch a good price as a private pet.

How thoughtless people were. They didn't consider how alien a setting a human home was for an orang-utan, but Sim and Lip knew. They had been trained to know.

As another wave of anger swept through her, she heard the sound of a vehicle approaching the Centre . . . and it didn't sound like their truck. Was it the ranger? She drew in her breath sharply, feeling a stab of fear.

She quickly slipped out of the day-nursery, locked the entrance and hid the key under a large stone. Then, she ran to the corner of the main building, from where she could see the parking area. A modern four-wheel-drive vehicle was being parked there. It wasn't the ranger's vehicle . . . and as the driver got out, she knew it wasn't Sim or Lip. This man was far too tall and seemed to be a European. As he stretched his arms above his head in a familiar gesture and slowly turned as he gazed about him, Jo stepped forward in amazement.

'Alec!'

He couldn't have heard her exclamation at that distance, but his eyes caught the movement of her body as she stepped into view.

'Jo! There you are, my love! Well, you've led me a pretty dance, haven't you?'

As he strode towards her, Jo's heart flipped. He'd come for her. In spite of her doubts, he'd come. Her heart beating rapidly, she ran towards him and laughed as he swept her up into his arms and swung her around in a complete circle.

She was still laughing when he set her down on her feet and covered her lips with his own. Her initial response deepened his ardour, but when Jo felt him kiss her more forcefully, she felt distinctly uncomfortable and she pulled away, laughing nervously.

Alec didn't release her from his arms and Jo placed her hands against his chest to give herself a bit of breathing space.

'Alec! What a surprise! You're the last person I expected to see here!'

'Surely not!' he smiled down at her. 'Isn't that why you told me where you were hiding?'

'I wasn't exactly hiding,' Jo denied breathlessly. 'I'm doing a photography project for Harry.'

'Ah, yes! Harry Bretherton! Trust him to put his oar in and attempt to capsize us all'

The truck returning drew Jo's attention away from Alec's face. For some reason, Jo didn't want Harry to see her being held so closely in Alec's arms and she wriggled free as Alec turned to face the truck.

Alec caught hold of her hand as she slipped from his arms and Jo found herself pulling him forward as she approached the truck.

'Look who's arrived!' she called to Harry with false gaiety in her voice as Harry got out of the truck, knowing Alec's arrival wouldn't be a pleasure to Harry. 'Just what we needed! Another man to help with the Centre!'

The two men exchanged a brief nod. As expected. Harry didn't look pleased at Jo's suggestion, but it was Alec who kicked it into touch.

'Whoa! Can't do it, I'm afraid! I only took a few days off work to fly out here. My return flight is booked for tonight.'

'Then why did you come?' Jo asked in amazement.

Alec lifted her hand up to his lips and looked deep into her eyes over the top of it. 'To ask you to marry me, of course! And . . . ' he quickly added, as the shock of his words made Jo instinctively try to jerk her hand out of his grasp, ' . . . to tell you that our esteemed uncle has had a bit of a relapse and wants to see you again . . . before . . . '

He let the end of his sentence drift in the air but Jo's mind instantly forgot the first part of his explanation and filled in the missing words . . . 'before he dies'!

'Oh, no!'

Her fingers flew to her lips as she felt a new wave of shock sweep over her. She felt filled with remorse that it might have been her action in running away that had caused his relapse. She turned to face Harry, her lips almost sound-lessly whispering his name.

'Harry!'

She wasn't sure why, but it was Harry's arms she wanted enfolded around her and Harry's voice speaking soft words of comfort and hope, but it was Alec who pulled her close again.

'So, get your things packed, my darling. We need to be on our way.'

'B . . . but I can't!' Jo stammered. 'There's only the two of us. There's been a bit of bother and our helpers have gone. I can't leave Harry to manage on his own. He . . . needs me!'

Tears pricked at her eyelids. She was torn between her loyalty to Harry and her loyalty to Uncle Willoughby. Both needed her, but she couldn't leave Harry on his own, not right now.

Harry came to her aid. 'It's all right, Jo. Your uncle needs you more than I do. The manager at Sepilok is sending two men over later today and I've alerted the ranger service. We'll be fully staffed by nightfall. You go with Alec.'

He spoke without emotion and Jo felt his words hit heavily, especially when he added, 'You've got plenty of photographs, so you'll be able to complete the project in the U.K., won't you?'

Feeling too choked to speak, Jo slipped out of Alec's grasp and ran indoors. She didn't care about the photographs. She didn't want to leave Harry at this dangerous time. She slowly placed her clothes into her suitcase and carefully packed her camera equipment and her laptop. When everything was stowed inside her baggage, she sadly joined Harry and Alec in the main living area.

'Surely one more day wouldn't make much difference?' she pleaded, her eyes more on Harry than on Alec.

Harry reached out both his hands to her. 'I'd rather you went. It'll be better all round,' he said softly. 'Go on. I'll be all right here . . . honestly.'

Alec briskly took her suitcase out of her hands. 'Come on. The sooner we leave the better.'

Jo still hesitated, her eyes beseeching Harry to say he needed her . . . and when he put his hands on her shoulders her heart leaped, but he turned her about and gently pushed her towards the doorway.

'Go on,' he said. 'You have to go. You'd never forgive yourself if you lingered here and were too late to see your uncle.'

Harry couldn't believe how devastated he felt as he watched the four-wheel drive disappear out of sight . . . and it didn't help to know that it had been the right thing to do. Jo had gone. Just like that. In less than twenty minutes his life had emptied.

Jo glanced over her shoulder as they reached the first bend in the track. Harry was standing immobile with his hands hanging loosely at his sides. Jo's heart lurched. She hadn't had time to say goodbye properly . . . nor to thank him for the wonderful opportunity he had given her. He'd be going round to the day-nursery soon to continue the daily routine with the juveniles. She ought to be there with him.

Alec concentrated on negotiating his way over the rough track, glad he had gone to the added expense of hiring a four-wheeled-drive. It lessened the impact of the bumps and hollows that were being continually remoulded by the regular downpour that were a feature of a tropical rainforest. He was also glad to have an efficient air-conditioning system in the vehicle.

He glanced sideways at the silent figure seated beside him, satisfied that she had come away with him so willingly. She'd soon forget that Bretherton bloke. Too dull by far.

Aware that he had laughed aloud, he added conversationally, 'I bet you'll be glad to get back to civilisation, won't you? I mean, it's all very well to come to these places for a holiday in a five-star hotel, but hardly the ideal place to go native!'

Jo was glad that Alec had allowed her time to compose herself before he spoke to her, but she found herself bristling at his blasé assessment of the centre she had grown to love.

'I liked it there!' she contradicted him. 'I'll miss it!'

'Hmm, if you say so, but I didn't even dare to think of the sanitary arrangements! Pretty awful, I should imagine. In fact, the first place we come to that looks as though it might meet the standard, we'll have to stop. I think I saw some bars just before I turned off the main road.'

Jo wondered why she wasn't ecstatically happy to be seated by Alec's side. He had come thousands of miles for her . . . and he had said he'd come to ask her to marry him, she retrospectively recalled. Wasn't that what she had always dreamed of?

Still, that prospect had to be weighed against the over-riding fact of Uncle Willoughby's relapse. That was the main concern in her heart. No wonder her reaction to Alec's appearance was subdued.

'Is he dying?' she asked quietly.

'What? Oh, Uncle Willoughby? I don't know.' He frowned through the windscreen giving the appearance of deep concentration on driving. 'It could go either way, I suppose. He was pretty bad when I left.'

'Oh, dear! It's my fault. I shouldn't have left like that.'

'Yes, it was pretty childish of you,' Alec agreed. 'What difference did it make to you and I? You knew I always intended to marry you. Uncle Willoughby's decision was just the icing on the cake. At least you had the sense to refuse Giles and Simon. Now, that would have scuppered us, wouldn't it!'

'I didn't know you always meant to marry me,' Jo said quietly. 'Why should I? You always had a stream of pretty girls on your arm.'

Alec grinned. 'Precisely! I wasn't serious about any of them. I was just biding my time. Like I told you the last time we met, I was waiting for you to grow up. And, if I may say so, you've grown up.'

Jo felt icy fingers clutch at her heart. Whatever was the matter with her? She should feel in seventh heaven!

'I'm sorry, Alec. I'm too worried about Uncle Willoughby right now, to think of us. Too much has happened too quickly.' She gave a nervous laugh. 'I can still hardly believe you're here.'

Alec reached out and squeezed her arm. 'I'm here, right enough! And, if I'm not mistaken, there's the main road coming up!'

They turned right towards Kota Kinabalu and shortly drew up outside a small cluster of buildings, one of which was a small store with a drinking bar at the side.

'I won't be long,' Alec said as he switched off the engine and opened the driver's door. 'Why don't you come with me and buy a few cans of something to drink while you're waiting? This heat is really getting to me. Have you got enough money?'

'Yes. I'll do that.'

She picked up her backpack and went with him into the store. Alec went through the bar, following directions to the toilets and Jo went over to a drinks cabinet, where she quickly selected a couple of diet-cola cans and a pack of bottles of water and took them to the man at the till.

As he rang up the prices, Jo casually glanced round and suddenly felt her mouth go dry. Through the open archway leading to the bar, she could see two men seated on high stools. The one facing her was European. She had never seen him before, but she was positive that the one with his back to her was Sim.

Taking the change from the shop-keeper, she silently moved into the archway and paused by a stand displaying a selection of packets of nibbles, Keeping her face turned away, she strained to listen to their conversation.

'So, you're sure there'll only be this

one Englishman and a girl there?' the European asked. 'And how many young orang-utans?'

'Eight . . . all younger than the one you got the other day and all used to being handled. You'll have no problems placing them.'

'Good. We might as well take all we can. When's the best time to catch them unawares?'

'Around mid-day. They'll be having lunch . . . and feeling the effects of the hottest part of the day.'

'Wouldn't it be better at night?'

Sim shook his head. 'No. They've put another lock on the night-nursery. I couldn't get in last night. The day-nursery is easier to get into.'

'Right. One more thing . . . are they likely to put up a struggle?'

'They'll resist at first, but they've no weapons. Wave a few guns around and they'll soon roll over.'

'Good. I'll see you out there.'

Jo swiftly dodged back into the store and darted round the back of the centre stand, hoping Sim didn't need to do any buying.

She was lucky. She heard the two men bid the shop-keeper goodbye, followed by the sound of the door closing. At the same moment, Alec reappeared coming through the archway back into the shop. Jo came out of hiding and grabbed his arm.

'Don't go out yet!' she hissed. 'Come round here! Remember I told you we've had a bit of bother? That man who's just gone out was the main cause of it!'

'So? You're well out of it, then!'

'No! You don't understand! I just heard them planning to go back to the centre to steal the rest of the orangutans. Harry's there on his own! And they talked about getting some guns. There's no way of warning him. We'll have to go back!'

Alec stepped back holding up his hands, palms forward. 'No way! We've a plane to catch, remember!'

Jo faced his resolutely. 'You'll be catching it without me!' she declared fiercely. 'I can't leave Harry to face this on his own. You've got to take me back! Please, Alec!'

The earnestness of her voice got through to him, but he tried once more to dissuade her. 'What about Uncle Willoughby? What if . . . we're too late?'

Jo hesitated only fractionally. 'Uncle Willoughby would understand. He'd put Harry's safety above a last glimpse of me! I know he would!'

'Maybe. OK, you win. But no more messing about after that. I want to get that plane.'

'Yes, I promise. Come on, we've given them time to get clear. Let's get on after them . . . and, I've just thought. The ranger gave us his number. I added it to my contacts list. If I ring him now, we're in range of a signal . . . as long as he is, too.'

Fortunately, he was and, although he was thirty miles away, he said he would organise some back-up forces and set everyone on the move. 'Do what you can to delay them getting away!' he suggested.

Jo next tried to contact Harry's phone, but wasn't surprised when she failed. Just in case, she quickly sent a text message. Anything was worth trying.

She was very much on edge as they drove back towards the Centre. They didn't know if the would-be thieves were ahead of them; nor how far ahead. Surprise would be their best weapon, so it was important not to be spotted until they were out of their vans.

Luck was with them. The thieves clearly had no idea that anyone might be following them and had made no effort to conceal their two vans, which they had parked a good way down the track.

'That's so Harry wouldn't hear them coming,' Jo commented. 'Is there any way to immobilise them?'

'If we can get at the engines. Yes, look, they've not even locked the doors. Ah, here's the catch. There, now, let's see what we can do.'

Jo watched anxiously as Alec disconnected the battery from the first van and then lifted it out and hid it in the undergrowth. As Alec had done the same to the second van, she grabbed Alec's arm to hurry him along.

All was quiet when they approached the centre. Whatever action had been taken was already over. Jo felt a clutch of fear reach her heart. Where was Harry?

11

Alec grasped hold of Jo's arm. 'Look, I want no heroics, Jo!' he warned. 'We are obviously outnumbered, so we're not going to win in a show of strength. No group of animals, however much endangered or appealing, is worth risking human life.'

'It's Harry I'm most concerned about,' she hissed. 'He was on his own here . . . so what's happened to him?'

'Where are the orang-utans?'

'Round the back.'

With a sense of shock, Jo realised Alec hadn't even gone to look at them when he was here earlier. Did he have no interest at all in what she and Harry were doing in the rainforest? With a wry grimace, she was forced to admit to herself that Alec never had been interested in what other people were doing.

Keeping a wary eye on the corner of the building in case the men appeared, Jo and Alec ran swiftly to the house and Jo led the way up the steps.

The main room was empty, with no sounds discernible, so they quietly entered. Jo ran silently over to the room the men slept in and saw at once Harry's gagged and bound figure lying on the floor.

She thought at first that he was unconscious but, as she hurried over to him with a faint cry of alarm, he opened his eyes and looked groggily at her.

The look of surprise mingled with hope and delight that lit Harry's eyes made Jo's heart lurch. Her mind froze for an instant as the enormity of her imminent departure from Borneo and Harry struck her afresh and it took a determined effort to distance herself from her thoughts and galvanise herself into action.

'I'll get a knife,' she hissed and cautiously ran to the small kitchen.

Flattening herself against the wall by the window, she peeped out, thankful that the mosquito netting hid her from view. She could see Sim and three other men inside the day enclosure and, as she watched, saw Sim raise his arm and point in the direction of the house.

She drew in her breath with a gasp, thinking he had spotted her, but, as she jerked herself aside, she realised he was pointing past the house and, when she risked another glance, she saw that two of the men were heading towards the house but, as one of them had taken a bunch of keys out of his trouser pocket, she guessed that Sim had sent them to get the two vans.

She sped back to the bedroom. 'Two of them are going back to the vans,' she said quietly, as she dropped to her knees beside Harry. She slashed the ropes that bound his wrists behind him first, so that he could begin to gently massage them, then his feet and, finally the gag.

'That leaves Sim and another man in

the day enclosure. What d'you think? Is it worth trying to overpower them? Go and peep through the kitchen window, Alec, and see what you think.'

She turned her attention back to Harry. 'How do you feel? We've immobilised their vans, so the other two will be back soon.'

Harry was struggling to his feet and clutched hold of Jo's arm as his ankles felt like giving way under him. 'Yes, Alec said what you'd done . . . and that the rangers are on their way.'

He took a few unsteady steps. 'The feeling's coming back . . . I'm OK. They took me completely by surprise and knocked me on the head, but I don't think I quite lost consciousness. Let's plan our action.'

Alec rejoined them. 'I reckon, if one of us approaches from where the other men are expected to reappear, that should grab their attention and it'll give the other two time to sneak up from behind and, hopefully, fasten them in. Have you got a spare lock handy

. . . one we can just snap on?'

'Yes, in the drawer in the desk. You know where, Jo.'

Jo quickly got it. 'Who'll be the best one to show themselves?' she asked. 'Shall I?'

'No, I'll do it,' Alec volunteered. 'As I'm a stranger, they won't immediately take fright. You two get ready to rush forward at their first moment of surprise.'

Harry and Jo agreed and they hurried outside, splitting in two directions to approach from different sides. Their plan worked. Alec's appearance startled Sim, but he turned to speak to his companion before stepping towards the open doorway. By that time, Jo had darted forward and pushed the sliding door into its closed position. Harry had the lock ready and he snapped it into place with a satisfied glare through the metal mesh at Sim.

The sound of running feet warned them that at least one of the other two men was on their way back to give the alarm to Sim. Harry, Jo and Alec drew back against the house wall, so that they weren't immediately apparent when the man dashed round the corner. As he ran forward, he realised that Sim and the fourth man were locked inside.

'What . . . ?'

He turned to run back but he spotted Harry and Alec and was momentarily halted. Harry and Alec launched themselves forward and brought him to the ground.

By the time they had hauled him to his feet, they could hear the roar of another vehicle approaching with speed. Hoping it was the rangers, they hustled the man around to the front of the compound, just in time to see another fleeing figure brought to the ground by a slim figure who had launched himself at his legs.

Jo instantly recognised Lip and felt immensely glad to see him. Three rangers spilled out of their Range Rover and swiftly took charge of the two defeated men.

'There are two more locked in the day enclosure,' Harry told them. 'They are secure for now . . . but I'll be glad to see the back of them.'

Lip approached them hesitantly. 'I'm sorry I let you down,' he apologised. 'Sim threatened to harm my family if I didn't join in with him . . . but I was not happy to help him. He is a bad man. He caused Mike's accident and these other man hauled the tree down on top of you when you first came here. He makes much money from selling the young orang-utans. I knew he meant to come back to take them all, but I could not get here in time to warn you.'

Harry held out his hand towards him. 'I'm glad you came back, Lip, and I'll be happy to have you back working here when everything has been sorted out.'

Alec slipped his arm around Jo's shoulders. 'I'm afraid Jo and I have to leave you.' He made great show of looking at his watch. 'We've a plane to catch and are cutting it pretty fine as it is.' He nodded at Harry. 'Glad to have been of assistance. Quite like old times, eh!'

'Yes. Thanks for coming back.'

Harry turned to Jo, his expression softening. 'And you, Jo. Let me know how you get on, won't you?'

She ran over to him and hugged him. 'I don't want to leave you, but we have to go. I promised.' She looked earnestly into his eyes. 'I'm glad I came. Thank you. It's been a wonderful experience. I . . . ' Her voice broke. 'Maybe I'll be able to come back?' she added in little more than a whisper.

Harry smiled sadly. 'Maybe,' he said quietly. 'But I don't think so.'

With a broken sob, Jo hurried over to Alec and they went quickly along the track to where they had parked their vehicle. Why hadn't she realised? She'd been a fool! There was so much she felt she had left unsaid . . . but there wasn't time.

Alec seemed exhilarated by the incident and lightly recalled the various moments as he drove out of the rainforest. He didn't seem daunted by Jo's lack of response and she was thankful that her brief replies were sufficient to keep him happy.

She was still very much subdued when they reached the outskirts of Kota Kinabalu and Alec banged the steering wheel with the flat of his hand when they were held up at a set of traffic lights.

'We're not going to make it,' he said flatly. 'Even if I didn't have to return this vehicle, we'd be pretty hard pushed. As it is, we've no chance.'

'The flight might have been delayed,' Jo suggested. 'Or maybe there's a later one. It was only a link-up to Kuala Lumpur, wasn't it? That's how we came?'

'There won't be another flight today. I chose the latest one, not knowing how much time I would have. We'll return the vehicle and then I'll get on the phone and see if we can transfer the air tickets to tomorrow and book into a hotel for the night. Is that all right with you?'

Alec left her seated in an air-conditioned lounge at the car-hire place whilst he signed the paperwork for the return of the four-wheel-drive and made a few phone calls to make the other necessary arrangements. When he returned to her, he was smiling.

'All done!' he announced. 'I've booked us in at the *Shangri-La* and a taxi to take us there. Come on. You're in for a bit of a treat. Just think . . . a shower, air-conditioning, a pool to swim in,' he murmured tantalisingly as he ushered her outside to where a limousine was already waiting for them.

The hotel was all that Alec had promised. Its spacious reception area overlooked well-kept gardens and there was a tantalising glimpse of the deep blue sea through the palm trees.

Jo stared around her as Alec went to the reception desk to book in. The subdued opulence of the place con-trasted so much with the simplicity of the accommodation at the orang-utan centre that she felt an overpowering wave of homesickness for the centre sweep over her.

The words that the receptionist was saying drew wandering attention. 'The room is ready, Mr Mattison and all the arrangements are made. Shall we say, in an hour's time?'

'Yes, that's fine,' Alec agreed, picking up the room key. He turned to Jo and took hold of her arm. 'I've booked a room overlooking the sea.'

'She called you Mr Mattison,' Jo said, puzzled. 'How come?'

Alec smiled. 'Ah! All part of a little surprise I've arranged for you. I'll tell you all about it when we're in our room.'

Jo stopped and faced him. 'Our room? Haven't you booked two rooms?'

'Ah, sweet little Jo! Don't worry. I'm not setting out to compromise you in any way. It's all part of the little surprise I mentioned earlier.'

Jo frowned. 'I feel too anxious

worrying about Uncle Willoughby to be wanting any surprises right now, Alec. Hadn't we better phone home to ask how he is and to let them know we've been delayed?'

'All taken care of, my love!' Alec smiled. 'I phoned from the car-hire place . . . and Uncle Willoughby is doing fine.'

Jo stared at him. 'You phoned home? Why didn't you tell me? You know how worried I am about him!'

Alec smiled teasingly. 'I thought I would tell you when we got here, as part of my little surprise. In fact, he said there was no reason for us to panic about getting home . . . so we could spend a few days here.'

Jo's thoughts were tumbling over each other. She didn't want to spend a few days here, lovely though it was. Malaysia to her meant the rainforest and the orang-utans and . . . and helping Harry at the centre.

'I think I'd rather go straight home, if you don't mind,' she said quietly. 'If

Uncle Willoughby was ill enough to make you come out here to take me home, then he's just putting a brave face on it. Did you speak directly to him?'

'Well, no . . . not exactly.' Alec sounded defensive. 'I spoke to that carer of his, Bretherton. He assured me that he's all right . . . and out of danger for the time being.' His tone changed as he added, 'Anyway, wait until you hear what my surprise is! I think you'll change your mind about rushing home.'

The porter had halted and was fitting his key into a door. He stood aside to allow Jo and Alec to step inside the room. Jo could see at once that it was a suite of rooms.

Jo glanced around without much interest. It just didn't feel right being here in the midst of all this opulence, when there was so much need out there in the rainforest.

'What d'you think?' Alec asked, sweeping his arm around the room.

Jo managed to force a smile onto her

face. 'Very nice,' she said lamely. 'So, what's this surprise?'

Alec tipped the porter and closed the door after him before turning back to Jo, grinning disarmingly, 'Today, Jo, you and I are going to be married . . . right here in this hotel.'

12

Jo stared at him appalled at his words. 'Married?' she echoed, sure that she had misheard . . . or misunderstood. 'But how . . . ?'

'Well, it did take a bit of forward planning,' Alec reluctantly admitted.

'But you didn't know you were coming. You can't have arranged it all today!'

Alec made a wry expression. 'Well, no. I was planning to come anyway. Uncle Willoughby's illness came just at the right time.' He shrugged his shoulders. 'It's no big deal.'

'But . . . the plane we missed?'

Jo had a flash of understanding. 'It's all been lies, hasn't it? I bet Uncle Willoughby hasn't had a relapse at all!'

'Of course he did!' Alec said unconvincingly. 'He's up and down by the minute. You know very well he could pop off at any time. Besides, why the big fuss? We're getting married! Isn't it what you've always wanted?'

He swept her into his arms and swung her around, kissing her on her lips as he lowered her back to the ground.

Jo froze, her mind buzzing with dishevelled thoughts. She put her hands against Alec's chest to push him away, but he held her too close. 'No, Alec . . . ' she protested. She didn't want this!

Alec smiled as he stroked a finger down her cheek and then laid it against her lips, shaking his head as if she were a silly girl not in her senses.

'Yes, Jo. You and me. In an hour's time we'll be Mr and Mrs Alec Mattison. I've changed my name by deed poll so that the family name won't disappear. We've got an hour to get ready . . . in fact there should be . . . '

He glanced around and tutted with annoyance. 'I've ordered a dress for you, something in cream silk. Hang on, I'll ring reception.'

As he stepped over to the phone that was situated by the bed, Jo's mind suddenly sprang back to life.

'Haven't you forgotten something?' she asked with a chill in her voice.

'Pardon?' Alec asked over his shoulder as he picked up the phone.

'My consent to all this,' Jo pointed out coldly. 'I always thought that a proper proposal and the bride's agreement were necessary before a wedding could be arranged.'

With a patronising expression on his face. Alec put the phone down and went back to where Jo was standing immobile where he had left her.

'Jo!' he laughed. 'You've wanted to marry me since you were in pigtails . . . and have followed me around like a little puppy with its tongue hanging out for years. You'll tell our children and grandchildren how I followed you half-way across the world to marry you. Still, if a proposal is what you want, a proposal is what you'll get!' He took hold of her hand. 'Dearest Jo, will you do me the . . . '

The telephone shrilled, cutting across his words.

He strode to the phone and picked it up. 'Yes?' he asked sharply. 'Oh . . . right! Yes, I expect my bank hasn't got my new details yet. There's no problem . . . Can't it wait? I just . . . Oh, all right, then. I'll be with you in two minutes.'

He replaced the receiver and swung back to Jo with an apologetic smile. 'Sorry about this! I'll have to return to reception for a minute to sort this out. Apparently, my bank details are still in my other name. They want a signature to fax through to my bank in England. Look, don't worry. I'll propose on bended knee as soon as I get back.'

'There's no need, Alec. I don't want to get married right now. It's too rushed. In fact, I'm not sure that I want to get married at all.'

'Nonsense. You've just got last minute nerves.' He looked at his watch. 'We'll have to be getting a move on. The registrar will be here soon. I'll chase up your wedding dress whilst I'm in reception.'

Jo opened her mouth to say, 'no', but Alec dropped a hasty kiss on her stunned lips and rushed away, leaving Jo to stare aghast at the closed door.

She now knew with certainty that she didn't want to marry Alec. She had been in love with a romanticised view of love and marriage and had kept it alive with her silly, empty dreams. In reality, she now realised, Alec meant nothing to her . . . apart from being her rather shallow, vain cousin.

Her legs felt as though they were about to give way and she sank onto the edge of the bed. What was she to do? She felt dreadful. Her refusal to go through with it would make him extremely angry.

Why all the secrecy and haste? The answer suddenly hit her . . . it wasn't just her he wanted. It was Uncle Willoughby's estate. He had flown out here to sweep her off her feet and marry her before she had time to think about it. And she'd believed him!

Well, it wasn't going to happen! She had to get away.

Harry had always been the one she turned to. He had never let her down. With a gulp of realisation, she knew it was Harry she loved! Always had! Only she had been too besotted with Alec to know it!

With a pang of regret, she knew she might have missed her chance with Harry. Had she snubbed his advances too often? He'd still help her, though.

She scrabbled in her back-pack for her mobile phone and hastily stabbed her way through to Harry's number. Was he in range of a signal?

To her amazement, Harry answered on the third ring. 'Harry! Oh, Harry!'

'Jo? Where are you? I'm on the outskirts of Kota Kinabalu. I'm looking for you.'

Jo found herself wiping a tear away from her eyes. 'How did you know?' she whispered.

'I rang home. Your Uncle Willoughby is as fit as a fiddle. I don't know what Alec's up to, but it's not to take you home to his dying bedside.'

'I know,' Jo gulped. 'He . . . he's arranged our wedding . . . me and him . . . within the hour. Oh, Harry, what can I do?'

After a slight pause, Harry spoke quietly. 'That's up to you, Jo. Isn't that what you always wanted? That Alec would ask you to marry him?'

'Yes . . . but not any more. He's rushing it through to inherit Uncle Willoughby's estate. I don't think he cares about me.'

'Where are you?'

Jo snatched up a brochure from the bedside table. '*The Shangri-La*. Tanjung Aru Resort. Keep on the coast road past the airport. Come quickly, Harry! I'll meet you in reception.'

She switched off her phone, her mind and body now poised for flight. She grabbed hold of her two items of luggage and swiftly crossed the room to the door. As she stepped out into the corridor, she saw Alec at the far end with a dress-bag over his arm. Her wedding dress, no doubt.

Hastily, she dodged back into the room and leaned back against the closed door. Could she keep him locked out? Maybe . . . but she needed to get to the reception to meet Harry. She'd have to leave via the patio window. Thank goodness they were on the ground floor.

She sped across the room, dragging her suitcase behind her and slid open the door. The hot, steamy atmosphere hit her afresh, but she barely noticed as she hurried along the path that ran alongside the building, heading in what she hoped was the direction of the reception.

A shout from behind her made her look over her shoulder. It was Alec . . . and, when he saw that she had no intention of stopping, he began to run after her.

'Jo! Stop!'

Jo darted through a gap in the building. It led back to the other side of the building, onto the open corridor that she knew led to the reception. She hurried on, knowing she needed to get to where there were other people, somewhere where Alec wouldn't want to make a scene.

She had almost reached the reception when Alec caught up with her. He grabbed hold of her arm and pulled her round. 'What are you doing? Why aren't you getting ready for the ceremony? I told you I wouldn't be long.'

Joe tried to jerk her arm free. 'There isn't going to be a ceremony!' she snapped. 'I'm not marrying you!'

'Look, if it's that silly proposal that's bothering you, I'll do it here and now!' Alec snapped back, dropping down onto one knee and keeping hold of her free hand. 'Jo, will you do me the honour of becoming my wife. I promise to love you forever and . . . '

'No. I don't want to marry you . . . especially not like this!'

'We'll just get engaged, then. We'll get married back in England. We can still have a holiday here. Look, just come back to our room and we can discuss it quietly. I'm sure you'll see the sense of it once you've thought it through properly.'

Alec struggled to his feet as two bemused hotel guests sauntered past. 'And what *is* the 'sense of it'?' Jo asked quietly. 'That you'll get Mattison Hall and all its land and tenancy rents?'

'What? No, of course not,' Alec blustered. 'You must have known I always intended to ask you to marry me . . . and you always made it pretty clear that you wanted me to. Why all this last minute playing about? Are you paying me back for all the girls I've taken out in the meantime? None of them meant anything to me, you know. They were just stop-gaps.'

Jo shook her head as more guests stepped around them, eyebrows slightly raised at the public quarrelling. Jo felt her cheeks burning.

'I don't care about the other girls. You've never made any secret of them. I've just discovered that I don't love you and, to be honest, I don't think you love me.'

'Of course I do!'

Alec tried to pull her closer, but Jo pushed her hand against him. 'It's no use. I'm not marrying you. I've phoned Harry and he's coming for me.'

'Oh! I might have known he'd be brought back into it! A snug little love-nest in the jungle, was it? Well, I'm here and he's not! And I've gone to all this trouble for you to back out at the last minute. I've got a special licence here and we're going to use it!'

'Not with Jo, you're not!'

Jo's heart leaped.

Harry was striding towards them, a couple of attendants from reception hurrying after him.

Alec's face glowered with anger. He thrust Jo from him and sprang at Harry, his fist drawn back to deliver a blow to Harry's head. Harry ducked, grabbed

Alec's arm and twisted his body around. Alec hooked a foot between Harry's legs and the two men crashed to the ground. As they fell, Alec landed a backward thrust with his elbow to Harry's midriff. Harry was winded but managed to deflect a blow aimed at his head. Alec tried again.

'Stop it!' Jo screamed, bending down and grabbing Alex's arm.

Alec used his strength to jerk his upraised fist back at Jo, knocking her sideways and freeing his left arm, but before he could resume his attack on Harry, a number of hotel attendants were on them, pulling them apart. Even then, Alec had to be forcibly restrained from lunging once more at Harry as he got to his feet.

The duty concierge appeared on the scene and the two men were unceremoniously hustled into a nearby side room. Jo followed them inside, going straight to Harry, who, although he was being held by two attendants, was not resisting their restraint.

'Are you all right?'

'I'll survive.'

'I'll kill you for this, Bretherton!' Alec snarled, attempting to lunge forward once more.

'Not in this hotel, you won't!' the concierge said grimly. 'And if you don't calm down immediately, Mr Mattison, in spite of the fact that you are a guest here, I shall have no alternative but to send for the state police.'

Fortunately, Alec had the sense to know that the concierge would do as he said and he allowed himself to be thrust into armchair, where he sprawled resentfully, still glowering at Harry.

The concierge turned to Harry. 'I don't know who you are sir, but you have stormed your way past security and I must ask you to leave the premises immediately if you, too, wish to avoid being questioned by the police. Any resistance . . . and I will have no hesitation in summoning them.'

'He came to rescue me!' Jo hastily explained. 'This man was trying to force me to marry him and I telephoned Harry to come and help me escape.'

'Hardly 'force you',' Alec sneered. 'You came with me willingly enough!'

'You tricked me! You said Uncle Willoughby was ill, but he isn't!'

Alec shrugged. ' 'All's fair in love and war!' ' he quoted off-handedly. He turned to face Harry. 'I suppose you'll be next one to try your luck?' he sneered. 'Just think, Jo, you'll never know whether it's you or your fortune anyone's after . . . and I'm not so sure you'd be worth it, anyway! She's all yours, mate!'

Jo flushed at the slight he offered.

Harry grimly took hold of Jo's elbow and ushered her from the room. She was thankful to leave Alec's presence, wondering why it had taken her so long to see the reverse side of his charm.

Harry grabbed the handle of her suitcase and strode out of the hotel, with Jo hurrying along at his side. She felt that everyone knew about the unseemly brawl and must be wondering what sort of person she was to have two men fighting over her.

Harry seemed no happier. He flung her suitcase into the back of the truck, opened the passenger door for her and helped here up and strode round to the driver's side. He wasted no time in starting the engine and driving away from the hotel and onto the public road.

'Thanks for coming, Harry,' Jo said quietly. 'I've been such a fool, haven't I?'

Harry glanced at her briefly and then returned his attention to the road. 'In thinking you were in love with Alec? In a word, yes! I'm glad you discovered your mistake in time. At least his indecent haste to marry you for Willoughby's estate showed him up for what he is.'

Jo twisted her fingers together, unsure whether to reveal the fullness of her realisation. What if Harry no longer cared that deeply for her? It was a risk she had to take. If he rejected her, she deserved it, she had rejected him often enough. But, at least she would know where she stood. She'd be able to catch a flight home to England and lick her wounds in private.

'I was having second thoughts before that,' she admitted quietly, biting her lower lip. 'As soon as I saw him, I knew how out-of-place he was . . . and even before he came . . . ' Her voice trailed off.

'Yes?' Harry queried. 'Before he came?'

They were out of town now. Harry glanced in the mirror and drew to the side of the road. He switched off the engine and turned sideways in his seat.

Jo blushed, reflecting how difficult it was to be the one to utter first words of a declaration of love when you weren't sure of the other's response. She took a deep breath.

'I was enjoying being with you. We've always been good friends, but it was different. You aroused feelings deep inside me that I'd never known before. That time in the pool . . . and other times. Just being with you. It made me realise that I didn't want to live anywhere without you.'

Harry took hold of hands. 'Even if marrying me means you lost Mattison Hall?'

Jo nodded. 'Even that!'

Harry grinned in delight. 'I can offer you a wooden chalet in the rainforest!'

'With no mod-cons?' Jo grinned back.

'None at all!' Harry agreed. 'Except a delightful forest pool, complete with a shower and running water!'

'I'll settle for that.'

'In that case, Jo Mattison, will you marry me?'

Jo sighed in complete happiness. 'Oh, yes!'

Later, when they decided to phone Uncle Willoughby whilst they were in range of a signal, they discovered another depth to her cousins' duplicity.

'Only inherit Mattison Hall if you

married one of your cousins, Jo?' she heard Uncle Willoughby's surprised exclamation. 'No, I told my nephews that my heir would be *whoever* you married! And I can't be more pleased that you've chosen Harry. Are you marrying him out there?'

Jo hesitated. 'Would you mind?'

'Not at all . . . as long as you come home soon so that I can give you both my blessing and throw a party for you. Be happy, Jo. I love you.'

'And I love you, Uncle Willoughby.'

Harry nuzzled into her neck. 'And me?' he whispered into her ear.

'Yes, and you!' Jo laughed . . . and sealed it with a kiss.

THE END

Other titles in the
Linford Romance Library:

TO LOVE AGAIN

Catriona McCuaig

Jenny Doyle had always loved her brother in law, Jake Thomas-Harding, but when he chose to marry her sister instead, she knew it was a love that had no future. Now his wife is dead, and he asks Jenny to live under his roof to look after his little daughter. She wonders what the future holds for them all, especially when ghosts of the past arise to haunt them . . .

FINDING THE SNOWDON LILY

Heather Pardoe

Catrin Owen's father, a guide on Snowdon, shows botanists the sites of rare plants. He wants his daughter to marry Taran Davies. But then the attractive photographer Philip Meredith and his sister arrive, competing to be first to photograph the 'Snowdon Lily' in its secret location. His arrival soon has Catrin embroiled in the race, and she finds her life, as well as her heart, at stake. For the coveted prize generates treachery amongst the rivals — and Taran's jealousy . . .

KEEP SAFE THE PAST

Dorothy Taylor

Their bookshop in the old Edwardian Arcade meant everything to Jenny Wyatt and her father. But were the rumours that the arcade was to be sold to a development company true? Jenny decides to organise a protest group. Then, when darkly attractive Leo Cooper enters her life, his upbeat personality is like a breath of fresh air. But as their relationship develops, Jenny questions her judgement of him. Are her dreams of true love about to be dashed?

LEGACY OF REGRET

Jo James

When Liz Shepherd unexpectedly inherits an elderly man's considerable estate, she is persuaded it is in gratitude for her kindness to him. But doubts set in when Steve Lewis, in the guise of a reporter, challenges her good luck. Was there another reason for her legacy? And why is Steve so interested? She comes to regret her inheritance and all its uncertainties — until Steve helps her find the truth and they discover the secret of their past.

RETURN TO HEATHERCOTE MILL

Jean M. Long

Annis had vowed never to set foot in Heathercote Mill again. It held too many memories of her ex-fiancé, Andrew Freeman, who had died so tragically. But now her friend Sally was in trouble, and desperate for Annis' help with her wedding business. Reluctantly, Annis returned to Heathercote Mill and discovered many changes had occurred during her absence. She found herself confronted with an entirely new set of problems — not the least of them being Andrew's cousin, Ross Hadley . . .

THE COMFORT OF STRANGERS

Roberta Grieve

When Carrie Martin's family falls on hard times, she struggles to support her frail sister and inadequate father. While scavenging along the shoreline of the Thames for firewood, she stumbles over the unconscious body of a young man. As she nurses him back to health she falls in love with the stranger. But there is a mystery surrounding the identity of 'Mr Jones' and, as Carrie tries to find out who he really is, she finds herself in danger.